THE GUARDIAN'S GIFT

THE GUARDIAN'S GIFT

**BOOK 3
IN THE SAGE CHEVAL SERIES**

SARAH FENLON FALK

Copyright © Sarah Fenlon Falk 2019

All rights reserved. No part of this publication may be reproduced, stored or transmitted in any form or by any means, electronic, mechanical, photocopying, recording, scanning, or otherwise without written permission from the publisher. It is illegal to copy this book, post it to a website, or distribute it by any other means without permission.

This novel is entirely a work of fiction. The names, characters and incidents portrayed in it are the work of the author's imagination. Any resemblance to actual persons, living or dead, events or localities is entirely coincidental

Cover design by cheriefox.com and Interior design by Richell Balansag

Be the first to know when the next book
in series is going to be released!
Go to www.SarahFenlonFalk.com and
sign up for email updates and more!

Thank you.
I can't offer a download for the next
book because it's not ready yet!

This book is for Grandma and Grandpa.

INTRODUCTION

From the Holy Scriptures:

"Peace I leave with you.
My peace I give to you."
John 14:27

From the Ancient Articles of Ploin:

If thou a Shalomite be,
Peace in all situations you seek.
A spirit of calm you present
Despite any word or act of descent.
If thou a Shalomite be,
Victory you may not always see.
No matter the situation of woe,
Peace alone will rule in your soul.

PROLOGUE

The Island of Drepos rested placidly off the northeast coast of The Kingdom of Monde's mainland. It was not inhabited year-round and because it was densely covered in trees, flowers and fauna of all kinds, it was known as the Garden Island.

This peaceful place was the only privately owned land in the kingdom. It had been in the same family for centuries. Though the king and queen of Monde did not possess the island, they did frequently visit the place in the summertime to picnic on its shores or to spend an afternoon exploring its foliage. The previous king and queen had enjoyed the place often, but the new king and queen were planning to make their very first visit to the island since their marriage almost a year prior.

The owner made sure he reached the island before they did. He and his daughter were prepared to make any necessary repairs to the dock or to cut away overgrowth so some of the more unique flowers could be accessed by the royal couple. The man's daughter was not a child. She was a grown woman. Since she remained unmarried into adulthood, she had chosen to stay with her father in the house she had grown up in. It wasn't until Princess Amalia had come from Estrella over a year ago that the woman found herself living at the Castle Grange as a lady of the queen. It had been a difficult transition for her but she loved the queen even though she did still worry about her aging father.

The island had always been a place where the gentleman's family had come to relax and enjoy the beauty of nature. It was especially nice in summertime and summer was indeed in full bloom on the island now. The young royal couple had picked the perfect time to make a visit to the Garden Island. They were sailing out in celebration of the approaching first-year mark of their reign.

The man and his daughter looked toward the mainland. The small ship bearing the royal party was nearing the island. Further in the distance the peaks of the Sommet Mountains were a backdrop of grays and white. There were few clouds in the sky on this sunny day.

The man stood as tall as he could while leaning gently on his cane and put a hand up to his brow to shield his eyes from the sun. Before long he was assisting with the disembarking of the royal party from their ship and onto the dock at Drepos.

"Welcome, welcome!" He said excitedly, bowing at the waist with each word. "King Elyon, Queen Amalia! May God bless your reign with many years and many children!"

With this he bowed and kissed the hand Queen Amalia had extended.

"Thank you, Sir Philip," she said with a smile.

She put her free hand on her growing belly that held the couple's first child.

He bowed again as they moved toward the sandy shore.

"Lady Dori!" Queen Amalia said when she saw the man's daughter, one of her ladies, standing on the shore, "Come, walk with me."

Lady Dori stepped forward and took the hand offered to her.

"Lady Dori," the queen began in her gentle voice as they walked through the sand toward a grassy area that eventually led to the forest. "This little one will be born soon."

Queen Amalia touched her belly with both hands and rubbed it, gazing down at it affectionately.

"Elyon will be such a wonderful father! And I am so happy to be a mother..." again the queen paused and Lady Dori waited for her to finish her thought.

"Lady Dori," Queen Amalia said, stopping in her tracks and turning toward the small woman, holding both of Dori's hands now.

"If anything should happen to me while I'm giving birth or after, I want you to be this child's guardian."

Lady Dori bowed in the sand before her queen, holding her hand and kissing it. She looked up into the queen's clear blue eyes and said with a raspy voice, "My beloved Queen, I will do what you ask."

CHAPTER ONE

Princes Robert and Theodore arrived at the docks at Falaise Bay late in the afternoon with Sir Logan and a couple other guards. The sun was already setting behind them as they stood facing east to the Beaumere Sea. The cliffs of the Sommet Mountains were beside them, casting their shadows over the port.

It was quiet on the docks now and the markets had long since shut down for the day but voices could be heard coming from the inn nearby.

"Crimson red with a black axe in the center," a rough voice was saying as the two princes entered the dining room area of the inn.

"That's what I saw," another man with a full beard confirmed, nodding his head so that his beard bounced.

When the group saw two of their princes and members of the guard standing in the doorway, they all stopped talking abruptly. There was a screeching of chairs and benches as the men stood and all bowed at the waist toward the young men.

"Good evening, gentlemen," Prince Robert began, "Please, return to your meals. We only wish to talk to you about what you have seen while at sea."

No one moved so he continued, "some disturbing reports have made their way to the castle and we are here to confirm their validity."

The men all nodded and most of them slowly returned to their seats and their food while others just stood and stared at the young princes. The room smelled like a mixture of beef stew and sweat and while remaining in the middle of the stuffy room was uncomfortable the princes stood their ground.

The large man with the large beard looked up at Prince Robert and Prince Theodore and tried to speak more softly, "I have seen the flag of the Oblager, your highness."

"Where did you see it, sir," Prince Robert asked at the same time Prince Theodore asked, "How many ships?"

The man bowed his head respectfully then looked up and said, "There were six ships I saw and all were nearly ten leagues from port."

A few other men at the table mumbled their agreement to this report.

"I see," Prince Robert confirmed, "thank you."

"My good men," Prince Theodore chimed, "how many ships are currently at port here in the Bay?"

Some suggested ten, others guessed nearly fourteen in answer to the prince's question. One man volunteered to run out and count for an accurate number. When he returned nearly twenty minutes later Prince Robert and Prince Theodore were seated at the head of a table each with a cup of warm drink in their hands.

The young man ran back in and reported to the princes on bended knee, "Your highness, there are twelve ships docked in the Bay."

Prince Theodore thanked him with a coin and a warm drink of his own.

Since darkness had fallen and the night was cold the princes decided to stay at the port for the evening. Rodney, a short, stocky man who the owned the inn as well as several of the ships currently in port, gave the princes the largest and best room on the second floor. Once the young men were certain Ardor and Honor had been fed and put up for the night the two of them retired to their room.

They could hear the continued conversations below, sometimes the voices sounded deep and rough, other times there would be peels of laughter that reached the second floor. Robert and Theodore tried to sleep.

Finally, Theodore turned over on his side facing his brother who was still wide awake in the other bed, "Are you planning to knight some of the sailors into the King's service and ask them to devote their ships to his kingdom's defense?"

Robert was quiet, but looked toward the sound of Theodore's voice in the darkness.

"What options do we have, Theodore? It seems like a battle at sea is the only option we have. We may not be able to hold them at sea from the shore for long."

"But these are merchant ships and fishing vessels. They are not outfitted with weapons of war," Theodore reminded him.

In the darkness the words hung heavy in the air.

Of course Theodore was right but Robert couldn't imagine any other way.

"We will have to provide them with weaponry then," Robert said. "And what we cannot find we must fashion."

Theodore was not surprised. He knew what this meant: the armory would have to be reopened. Despite the knowledge of the many tasks that awaited them in the days to come, the two princes allowed the sound and rhythm of the waves crashing into the cliff below to finally lull them to sleep.

CHAPTER TWO

The sun had begun to set behind the Wild West Wood by the time Lady Dori reached her destination. Serenity had ridden hard and had gotten them where they needed to go before the last light. Lady Dori's head had been so full of thoughts and plans after hearing that the Oblager ships were reaching the bay that she hadn't taken a moment to enjoy the familiar surroundings.

The village of Ploin was the farthest village from the Castle Grange. It was where Lady Dori had grown up. She had served Queen Amalia and then King Elyon since she had left her father's home. All of her childhood, all of her life but the last sixteen years, had been spent here in the village near the mountains. Serenity stopped before the thatched gate and Lady Dori dropped to the ground. Both were weary from the ride but knew it was a necessary trip nonetheless.

Quietly, Lady Dori opened the gate and led Serenity to the side of the house where a straw awning provided shelter for the horse that belonged to the man of the house. The plain brown mare was tethered to a pole with a bunch of hay set before her. The horse bucked her head in acknowledgement but she did not speak, for she could not. This mare was a quartier, a horse that needed to be cared for, not one of the wild and free Sage Cheval. Serenity spoke softly to the horse and acknowledged her.

Before turning for the house Lady Dori pressed her forehead to Serenity's for a moment in prierie. After their pause for connection Lady Dori turned toward the home. Putting one foot in front of the other on the stone path to the door of the cottage she soon reached the door. There she paused.

She put her palm to the door as if feeling for its heartbeat. It had been so long since she had come home. She loved this home, loved her father, and knew the question she must ask him now could be confusing for him. She would have to trust that he would understand.

She raised her fist but before she could knock or reach for the knob the door was opened. A middle-aged man with dark hair and a kind smile welcomed her.

"Lady Dori," he said with a bow of his head. "You are home!"

"Yes, thank you, Joseph."

"Your father is in here," he said and led her into the next room where her father sat with his legs elevated onto another chair and a heavy blanket laid over them. He was sitting beside a small fire and seemed to be dozing but when she touched his shoulder he opened his eyes without moving any other part of his body.

A smile crept across his round face.

"My girl!" He finally said, "I have missed you!'

Lady Dori sat in the chair nearest him, grabbed up his hand and kissed it. He turned his head toward her, a smile still on his lips.

"And I have missed you, father. How are you? You look well."

Joseph brought in two mugs of tea and left the two alone to talk privately.

Lady Dori looked into her leather bag and pulled out the journal and map.

"Father," she said, ensuring his eyes were upon her as she spoke, "there is a serious matter I need to discuss with you and we haven't much time."

He stared at her patiently, the flames from the fire lighting the side of his wrinkled face. He shifted in his seat to sit up more, to show his attention.

"Here is the map and the journal you gave me. I have some questions about them, but first, I need to know: will you grant me my inheritance now, even as you live?"

The old man sat quietly. If he was confused or concerned his face did not betray it. After only a moment he touched his daughter's hand.

"What are your plans, my child?"

"Father, I wish to offer the Isle of Drepos to the Oblager people as a land where they can settle and make a life for themselves."

Sir Philip tilted his head up and slowly nodded his understanding.

"I see. And have you discussed your plan with Prince Robert or the Doyen?"

Lady Dori shook her head. "I had to see you first, to know if it was mine to give."

Her father's smile widened and the wrinkles in his cheeks and next to his eyes deepened.

"Dori, you may have the island to do with as you wish. You know that I trust you as well as you know that I would do anything for Prince Robert, King Elyon and the Kingdom of Monde."

"I do, Father," Dori spoke with tears streaming down her face. "I do know it. I only hope this works."

After wiping his daughter's cheeks with both hands the man laughed.

"No one has dared try something like this ever before!"

Dori smiled too and chuckled, "Perhaps that it is why I believe it will work!"

The night did not pass peacefully at Castle Grange. The news of the Oblager ships on the horizon had startled everyone. The threat of their arrival had been real but so distant that the youngest royal children didn't think it would ever happen. And now that it had...

"Robert has shown himself capable of things even *he* never thought he could do," Margaret was saying, "I fully believe he will meet this challenge."

"But this could mean *war*," Samuel said, shaking his head and turning back toward the fire to warm his hands. "What do any of us know about that?"

"We will provide all the assistance that is within our power," Sir Edward said reassuringly.

"We have seen war before, Prince Samuel," Sir Francis added. "And we have seen the Kingdom of Monde prevail!"

"I wish father were here," Lillian said barely loud enough to be heard. She was seated in a chair nearest the fire, her head resting on the side of it. She looked weary and to this point hadn't said a thing.

Margaret went to her and put a small hand on her shoulder.

"Me too."

"Of course we *all* do," William said, "but he's not here and so we have to figure this out."

He put his head down on his arms in exasperation as he sat at the table.

"We won't be able to figure anything out tonight," Lady Claire said as she entered the room and began to put out the fire. "Come now, I've put cups of tea by each of your beds. Please do try to get some rest tonight. You will need it."

With that she shooed all of the young princes and princesses off to their chambers for the night.

CHAPTER THREE

It was late afternoon the next day by the time Lady Dori and Serenity returned to Castle Grange. After some time in prierie Lady Dori left Serenity with the other Cheval and went out to meet Prince William. She knew he would be at the dovecote. The round stone building housed the king's doves that were trained to send messages throughout the Kingdom of Monde. It was Prince William's responsibility to check for messages and to tend to the doves. She knew he enjoyed this task very much and would take his time there.

Prince William walked around the building to the small opening and jumped when he saw Lady Dori.

"You surprised me!" He said with a smile. He had to take a deep breath to calm his nerves.

Lady Dori blushed and bowed her head, "I did not mean to startle you, Prince William. I would like to speak with you and knew you'd be here. I've been waiting."

"Checking the dovecote for messages won't take me long. Can we talk when I'm finished?"

Lady Dori nodded and sat on the stone bench next to the garden wall near the dovecote. Prince William was at her side in only a few moments.

"I have been thinking about the Oblager," Lady Dori began.

"The Oblager have definitely been on all of our minds, Lady Dori," Prince William said.

"Yes. But I think we should take a different approach with them than anyone has ever dared."

Prince William tilted his head to look sideways at the woman, his eyebrows raised in curiosity. The lady was small in size and stature. She was barely taller than soon-to-be eleven-year-old Prince William.

Lady Dori seemed to be organizing her thoughts and the cooing of the doves filled the silence in the air.

Then she finally said, "Perhaps we could send a dove to their ship and invite them to come to the port, to Falaise Bay."

Prince William's brows fell into a furrow, "Forgive me, Lady Dori, but I do not see the wisdom in that."

"It would be for a purpose, my prince. We would invite them to come and to talk. If they were given the opportunity to share what it is they seek, what they want on these shores, perhaps we could provide it to them without incident?"

Prince William's shoulders relaxed and he exhaled. He hadn't realized he was holding his breath, but indeed he had been. It wasn't a surprise to feel such tension. Everyone had been a little tense since the reports of the Oblager ships first came to them.

Lady Dori smiled and turned toward him. "Perhaps we could give them what they need and be waving goodbye to their departing ships just in time for your birthday celebration!"

Prince William smiled back at her. It was a nice thought. He wasn't sure how realistic it was, but it was a nice thought nonetheless. Still, he wondered if it was an idea that Robert might be interested in.

So the Prince William said, "Let's go and talk to Prince Robert and the Doyen together. If there is a chance to appease the enemy without having to fight them we should take it!"

The afternoon sun shone down on the hillside warming Lillian and Margaret who had ridden out to the little brown cottage so early that the chill of the morning had clung to them as they worked to clear away debris from around the outside of the place. Temperance and Delight had taken shelter under the nearby trees when the sun made its way high into the sky.

The cottage was neatly situated on the side of a hill near the village of Colline. It had become a special place to Margaret recently as many of her earliest memories had been restored to her there. She was determined to rebuild the home that had once been a sheep farm and the favorite getaway of her parents. She wanted to give it new life and purpose.

"Maybe we should take a break?" Lillian suggested. "We've been at this a while and I think it is looking much tidier!"

Margaret continued to throw boards and debris from the house into the pile they had created. She glanced at her sister then at the cottage and shrugged. "Yeah, it looks a little tidier but there's still so much to do be done. I don't think I can rest until I see much more improvement."

Lillian wiped her brow with her sleeve. The work was hard and the sun was warming them even though fall was rapidly approaching.

"I for one need a rest," Lillian said, sitting down in the grass near where Temperance stood.

She rubbed one of the horse's legs and smiled. "Ah, this shade is perfect."

Margaret continued her work without acknowledging her sister's remarks. This was not surprising and Lillian's smile widened as she thought, *my sister is back… headstrong and focused!*

Delight looked over at her girl and huffed, stomping a hoof lightly to get her attention. Margaret looked up immediately and nodded her consent. The special bond between a Sage Cheval and their companion is deep. This connection is formed through times of prierie, a time when no words are needed to communicate the thoughts and feelings of animal or human. Margaret knew what Delight meant without a word spoken and she went to be near the Cheval.

"You are right," Margaret said, putting her head against her companion's flank. "I'm getting all caught up in this project again. I will rest."

After a silent pause with Delight, Margaret went and sat near Lillian.

"We are about ready to bring in the builders, don't you think?" Lillian said.

Margaret shrugged. She had seen the cottage in her dreams, daydreams *and* during the night, and she knew what the place should look like once restored. What she was looking at now seemed a far cry from what it *should* be.

"There's not much more here on the ground that we would be able to clear out," she explained when Margaret said nothing.

"We should go inside and clear things out. I could show you where I saw our mother…" Margaret's voice trailed off. She hadn't shared her visions, her dreams, her memories with her siblings for fear they would think she was crazy. It had been almost two weeks since she had had any vivid dreams. The celebration she had arranged for her mother, bringing Queen Amalia's life and memory back into Castle Grange, had changed her. She no longer remained deep in her grief. She still longed for her mother but no longer dwelled on the loss, but rather focused on the things her mother had given to her: life, love, and a strong spirit.

Lillian gently touched her sister's arm, breaking into her thoughts, "Margaret. Show me."

Samuel and Endurance were finishing a time of prierie together when Theodore and Robert returned from their night in Falaise Bay.

The two returning princes paused for a moment of prierie with their Cheval as well.

The afternoon sun streamed into the stables. The smell of fresh hay and straw thickened the air. All was quiet as the young men paused to deepen the connection with their Cheval.

When they turned to leave the stables Robert put an arm around Samuel and said simply, "the reports have been confirmed."

With a nod Robert and Theodore headed toward the castle.

Prince Samuel stopped and stood silent. The muscles in his back and neck were tense. He could feel his hands start to sweat and wiped them on his pants. Endurance could sense the frustration and inclined his head toward his young man, inviting conversation. Samuel knew what Endurance was asking: why are you frustrated?

Samuel put a gentle hand on Endurance's muzzle, acknowledging his concerns. "I have plenty to say to them," Samuel said, "but I feel like no one asks for my opinion; no one listens when I do speak."

"My young man," Endurance said, "it is important for you to share your ideas. Your input is valuable."

"I'm not so sure about that," Samuel replied. "But I thank you for the encouragement all the same."

Endurance remained silent. He knew his young man was not yet ready to hear what the Cheval would say. Nor was the young prince ready to share the words on his heart and mind. There was more the young prince would need to learn before he would be truly ready to speak.

CHAPTER FOUR

All four princes sat with Sir Edward and Sir Nelson in their study, high in the tower of the Castle Grange that afternoon. The sunlight that streamed in through the tall windows was turning a dark orange as evening approached. The light was sufficient and illuminated the maps unrolled on the tables in front of them. Large books with writing and drawings from ages past lay open on the large tables as well.

"We have men at the armory right now preparing it for production," Prince Theodore said.

Prince Robert nodded and said, "The king's guard has added to its numbers. The men are in the watch towers as well as commissioned throughout the kingdom to prepare the villages."

After a moment or two of silence, Prince William stood and cleared his throat.

Everyone looked at him and he smiled and shrugged slightly before saying, "I wanted to tell you all something. I - a - a conversation I had with Lady Dori. She suggested to me that perhaps we should invite the Oblager into port for a meeting. Perhaps to negotiate a peace, depending on what their purpose is here. What do you think?"

William assumed he *knew* what they were thinking as both Samuel and Theodore had jumped out of their chairs at the words "invite the Oblager into port". Sir Edward and Sir Francis had raised eyebrows but said nothing.

It was Sir Francis who was the first to speak. "It is not such a preposterous idea," he said. "Even if it only serves to buy us more time to prepare. Lady Dori is no stranger to negotiations. If she suggested it she must have an idea or perhaps some sense about the Oblager's willingness to talk?"

"Sir Francis, have you ever known the Oblager to stop and *talk*?" Prince Theodore asked, still standing.

"No, Your Grace. They have not been known to stop and talk," Sir Edward answered for his colleague. "However, they have *never* been invited to do so; at least not that I am aware of."

"Perhaps the very gall of it will confuse them for a bit?" Prince Robert suggested.

"Perhaps."

Prince Samuel walked over to Prince Robert, put an arm around his shoulder, leaned in as if he were about to share a secret and said softly, "You're not seriously considering this, are you?"

Prince Robert looked over at his wise men. The two men motioned back at the prince with a bow, deferring the final decision to him.

"If it has not been done before then perhaps it is in our favor to try. And if Lady Dori herself has experience in negation and peacemaking then that is also to our benefit. Wouldn't you say, brother?"

With that being said, Prince Robert looked at Prince Samuel waiting for his response. The young boy bowed his head without looking up, his dark hair covering his eyes.

Prince Robert hugged him tighter. "We must try something. We are no match for the Oblager on land or at sea."

Prince Samuel nodded in agreement and locked eyes with his brother finally, "You are right. We must try."

"I'll send a dove then?" Prince William asked, rising to his feet as if he were already on his way.

Prince Robert nodded.

It was when all the royal children were seated at the dinner table that the brothers decided to share their idea of extending a peace offering to the Oblager. Their sisters were not pleased to hear it.

"Do you think inviting the enemy onto our shores is the best plan?" Princess Lillian asked, wiping the corners of her mouth and placing the napkin onto her lap.

"I understand your concern. We are all concerned," Robert said, "but we want to try something different. No one has ever invited the Oblager to their lands. What if a peaceful solution can be found? Shouldn't we try?"

Lillian shrugged slightly and nodded, even as she rolled her eyes.

The plan did make sense, yet the idea was frightening and she couldn't find peace within herself about it.

"We won't bring them into the villages or to the castle," Robert clarified. "We will meet out at the port. You and the ladies will stay here while we will go out, under heavy guard, of course."

"Will all of you be going?" Margaret wanted to know. "I mean, what if something happens and Lillian and I are here alone?"

Lillian let out a sound and looked at Margaret, eyes wide.

"Well?" Margaret said defending herself. "We don't know, do we?"

"You won't be alone," Robert corrected her. "You will have guards, the ladies, Lord Nelson-"

"And I will stay with you," William said.

"And William," Robert finished, with a slight smile at his youngest brother.

"And you will return home as soon as the meeting is over so that we know you are alright?" Lillian asked.

"Yes, we will do our best to return as soon as our discussion with the Oblager is over. You won't need to worry."

"Well, if Sir Francis and Sir Edward are behind the plan then I will attempt to find some peace about it,"

Lillian said finally. "I don't think they would ever let you do something that they didn't think had at least a fair chance of success."

With that, the discussion was closed.

And it did not matter whether the young royals were set on the plan or not, for as they finished their dinners, the dove Prince William had released earlier that day was making its way to Falaise Bay, the Beaumere Sea and to the ships of the Oblager.

CHAPTER FIVE

It wasn't Prince Samuel's primary task, checking for messages at the dovecote, but for the next couple of days he found himself standing at the arched doorway peering inside and watching for any dove that would come to rest on the perching stand in the middle of the room. The doves had been trained to rest there if they were carrying a message. Patience had never been one of Prince Samuel's strengths and he could admit as much. It wasn't that he didn't trust William to do the job correctly either. It was just that he found it so difficult to sit and wait that he had to, yes, *had to* return to the dovecote a number of times each day. And so it was on the third day after the message from the castle had been sent to the Oblager, that Prince Samuel was the one to retrieve the message.

It was just before the midday meal and the young prince knew his siblings would be gathering in the dining hall. He wasted no time in reaching the castle, breaking into the great room and running with long strides into the dining hall where his siblings were, as he had imagined, already seated in their places.

He held the message up over his head and yelled, "This is it!"

Robert ran to him in an instant and grabbed the paper out of his hand.

"It says they wish to meet!" Robert said triumphantly.

"They wish to meet?" Lillian repeated as if she were not sure she had heard the words correctly.

The older three brothers were patting each other on the back and repeating "they accepted our invitation" and "they wish to meet" to one another while William, Lillian and Margaret remained seated at the table.

Finally, it was Theodore who stopped the celebration abruptly. He looked at his brothers, his arms still around both of them.

"They wish to meet. Now what?"

"I was so certain they would *not* want to meet that I haven't even been thinking in that direction," Robert admitted. "But since they have accepted the invitation we know what we must do."

It had already been arranged. It was all guesswork, however. No one had anticipated the Oblager would actually accept the invitation to a meeting for negotiation on the shores of Monde. What did this wayfaring people like to eat? What kind of accommodations would they expect? So little was known about the Oblager, even Sir Francis and Sir Edward seemed to be timid in giving their advice.

No one at Castle Grange had imagined that the white tent that had sheltered the celebration of Queen Amalia's life just several days before would be used to shelter a group of sailors off the coast of the port at Falaise Bay. Yet there it was the very next day, set up on a hill overlooking the port town.

Early that morning, after a group of soldiers had worked to raise the massive white tent, Sir Logan and some of his men had arrived at Castle Grange to escort the small contingency that would be needed in the talks with the Oblager.

As they left through the castle gates Prince Theodore leaned over to Prince Robert to whisper in his ear, "Do you really think Lady Dori should be coming? Isn't it safer for *all* of the women to stay at the castle?"

Prince Robert looked over his shoulder at the small woman seated astride her Sage Cheval, Serenity. A large leather pack was thrown over her shoulder and the strap gripping her chest somehow made her look even smaller.

"This was all her idea and she wanted to come," Robert answered his brother. "She actually told me that she *needed* to come. The Doyen said she has experience in peacekeeping so she could prove to be very valuable in this exchange."

Prince Theodore shrugged and shook his head. "I truly hope that is the case."

When the group reached the tent high on the cliff overlooking the port at Falaise Bay, the flags that proudly waved atop the large masts of the Oblager ships could already be seen in the water below.

"They arrived into port before the first light," one of the guards told Prince Robert. His name was Elijah and his mission was to guard Lady Dori. He had been standing guard at the port all night but was alert and ready.

Lady Dori dismounted her Cheval and after a moment in prierie Elijah was there, taking up his post close beside her. She looked up at him and smiled, then walked toward the tent. The young man followed close behind her, keeping his head up and his eyes sharp. Lady Dori understood his task and determined not to make his job more difficult than it had to be.

The delegation from the dark and formidable ships of the Oblager could be seen unloading onto the docks below them. Prince Samuel, Prince Theodore and Prince Robert were standing at the base of the mountains near the tent. From high on their vantage point they could make out the number of figures that were now walking on the road up toward their meeting point. One figure seemed much larger than the rest but they all looked very small from this distance.

Prince Samuel let out a breath as if he'd been holding it the entire hour since his arrival at the port. He looked behind them toward the tent and saw the small woman sitting in the middle of it. She looked so tiny.

"Are we sure about having Lady Dori here?" Samuel said to his brothers. Concern furrowed a line into his brow as he looked back at the row of men who were becoming larger and larger the closer they came.

Sir Edward, who had been keeping watch nearby, came to stand near the princes.

"Forgive me, Prince Samuel, I could not help but overhear your concern for Lady Dori. I believe it is important to tell you: she is a Shalomite. She is no stranger to peace talks or negotiation and is known for bringing peace into situations."

This did not seem to put the young prince at ease, but he did not argue his point any further.

Prince Robert turned and walked back under the tent. He approached Lady Dori and put an arm about her shoulders. At nearly fifteen years of age the prince stood a head and shoulders taller than the slight woman.

"Are you ready?" He asked her.

She nodded and her soft silver hair bobbed with the movement. She had a small smile on her thin lips and her eyes twinkled as if she knew something he did not. She was so calm and quiet that had Prince Robert not invited her here himself he might have missed her. But one thing that made her remarkable was the peacefulness she emanated – it was so welcoming.

Moments later the men from the ships had reached the ledge where the tent stood, the white and blue flag of the House of Rosh, complete with the image of the Cheval; the elements of earth, air, wind and sky flapped in the wind above them all.

Prince Robert walked out to meet the Oblager delegation and invite them into the tent where they would be meeting. Lady Dori could hear grunts and deep voices saying, "very well" and "as you wish." In a moment the men were filing into the tent.

As had been agreed upon, Elijah stepped forward. He was in his full metal armor and had a sword at his side. It was not drawn, but his right hand rested on the hilt lightly as if to say, "I'm ready." While Lady Dori felt she needed no such protection she knew some of the royal house had felt it necessary to increase weapon and manpower, and so, here he was.

Lady Dori put her shoulders back and chin up. She stretched to stand her full height in the presence of the men. It wasn't until the last man entered the tent that Prince Samuel thought he saw her flinch a little. The man had to duck to get his head inside the tent. He seemed to be as big as their dovecote at Castle Grange. He had a thick black beard and thick dark eyebrows to match. It seemed the earth trembled under the weight of his steps. He was more than twice the size of Lady Dori, a match-up which reminded Samuel of David and Goliath. But when Samuel looked again, Lady Dori stood as straight as ever with that quiet look on her face, eyes fixed on the group of men before her. He shook his head in wonder and went to stand at Lady Dori's side.

Inside the tent, cushions and lounge chairs had been provided for the group, as well as some chairs set around a table at the front of the tent. Sir Francis, who had also insisted upon attending, said that he would serve the drinks and refreshments to the men. True to his word he stepped forward now with a pitcher of fresh water in his hands.

Lady Dori was the first to address the group. "Please, make yourselves comfortable," she said and gestured to the cushions and lounge chairs. Most of the men from both delegations took a seat. One young man with a thin physique and strong arms stood near the back of the tent, one hand on his sword. It looked as though his arm muscles were flexed. He kept looking all around the tent, as if counting the number of men or considering whom he would attack first if it came to it. There were several men standing near him. All of them seemed younger than those seated at the table across from the three young princes.

The man with the short white beard who seemed to be one of the older men of the group and the one who was clearly the leader snorted when Princes Robert, Theodore and Samuel sat down across from him.

"You are just boys!" He said, spitting out the words.

With a tilted chin and an air of confidence the acting King of Monde said, "I am Prince Robert of The House of Rosh, ruler of the Kingdom of Monde. We have invited you here in hopes of forging a path to peace between our people and yours."

"A path to peace?" The man asked and then snickered, looking around at the other Oblager men who also laughed at the comment.

"We wish to extend peace to you and are willing to provide whatever it is you seek on these shores if we are able to obtain it."

"It's not half as fun if it's freely given," a man at the back of the tent said and laughter rose among the group once again.

Princes Robert, Theodore and Samuel remained calm. Even though their instincts were telling them to run, they didn't so much as shift in their seats. What the young princes lacked in confidence in the face of the men mocking them, they made up for in determination as they sat quietly.

Laughing one moment and staring at the young princes with a stern face the next, the older man said more slowly this time, "What makes you think we would accept anything from you?"

This time no one laughed.

The young princes remained silent.

What good is all of this back and forth? Why had they accepted the invitation if they didn't wish to talk? Prince Robert thought. While things seemed to be a bit chaotic he wasn't convinced that trying to take control of the meeting would be the best approach.

Prince Theodore leaned over to Robert and whispered in his ear. "If they don't want anything from us, why are they here, in our waters?"

Prince Robert sat up straight in his chair with a loud cough.

That proved to be enough to demand attention and soon all eyes were on him.

"If you do not wish to accept anything from us, that is fine. But we have invited you here as a gesture of peace. We would like to know what it is you *do* want and need, in hopes of being able to provide it," the young prince said, sweat beading on his brow.

There was a grunt at the back of the tent.

The old man narrowed his eyes and leaned forward to stare at the young prince.

He looks like a cunning fox, Lady Dori thought as she stood still with a guard on either side of her. *What is it you want, fox?*

CHAPTER SIX

On the hillside near Colline Princess Lillian and Princess Margaret were on their way back to the brown cottage. Lillian was trying hard not to think about the peace talks that were taking place at this very moment on the cliffs near Falaise Bay.

"You know I'm not typically one to worry," Lillian said to her companion, Temperance, "but I cannot get the threat of the Oblager out of my mind for some reason."

Temperance did not speak but waited for her girl to continue.

"I am unsettled by their presence. The sooner I watch their ships sail away, the better."

Temperance huffed her understanding.

"I'd love to get a peek at them," Margaret breathed.

"What?" Lillian snapped and looked hard at her younger sister. "It's bad enough our father isn't here to conduct the talks with our enemy; that our brothers are there instead. And now my only sister wants to head off and 'get a peek at them'? Don't you even think of it, Margaret!"

When Margaret did not answer or even acknowledge her sister, Lillian repeated, "Don't – even – think - about it!"

"Alright, Lillian," Margaret mocked. "Why are you so anxious? They haven't done anything to us."

"Yet," Lillian added. "Not yet. But we can't be so foolish as to think this couldn't lead to trouble."

"Let us not lose sleep over it," Temperance said. "Do not borrow worry from tomorrow, for today has enough trouble of its own. It will take all of our attention to live out *this* day."

Lillian leaned in toward Temperance's neck and whispered something to her then sat up tall.

Living out this day meant that the two princesses and their Cheval would be clearing the rest of the debris from within the house in preparation for the artisans of the village to come and restore the place. It was hard work but the girls did it without complaint. It wasn't hard for Lillian to imagine how inviting and sweet the cottage could or would be once their work was complete and the artisans had a chance to apply their expertise to the place.

Delight and Temperance were on hand to lend their strength and support to the task. While a Cheval was too respected in the kingdom to be simply used for manual labor, the Cheval themselves often offered to work alongside their companions in this way. Delight and Temperance proved to be invaluable to the job that Lillian and Margaret were trying to accomplish and before the end of the day the house had been completely cleared of all debris.

Before heading back to the castle the four of them sat under the shade of the nearby trees. Night was coming sooner than usual and it was clear that fall was quickly approaching.

"I am so looking forward to going into this place when its been restored," Margaret said breathlessly.

She was imagining what it had been like to live the memory of her mother and father at the table inside the cottage. They had been laughing and sharing a meal with Lord Riley and his wife. Since that couple had died from the plague that killed Queen Amalia, the sheep farm had been left abandoned and had fallen victim to the elements, time and weather.

"I wonder why the Lord Riley who came to our courts not long ago did not want to take care of this place when his brother died," Margaret thought out loud.

"Perhaps the pain of the memories in this place bring is too great for him," Delight suggested.

After sitting in silence a bit longer it was decided they should return to the castle before darkness fell. As they packed up to go it was clear to Delight that her girl was still thinking.

"What is it?" Delight asked.

"I'm still wondering about the young Lord Riley. I would really like him to see this place. Perhaps after the artisans have done their work I will invite him here."

"That is a good idea, my girl. Give him the option to come or not. But it would be good for you to guard your expectations should he choose not to come."

While Margaret couldn't fully understand why Lord Riley wouldn't want to come once the place was fully restored she determined to keep her hopes tamed, just in case.

CHAPTER SEVEN

The group of Oblager stood near the rear of the tent at a distance from the table they had been seated at just moments before. The attempts at negotiation for peace on the part of Prince Robert and his family seemed to be going nowhere and the young prince was visibly flustered. His pale cheeks were flushed, even though there was a cool breeze being swept up the side of the cliff from Falaise Bay and making its way through the tent. He tried not to continually wipe sweat from his brow, but it was there, glistening in the light of the setting sun.

"We haven't accomplished a thing," Prince Theodore said to his brothers, Lady Dori and the guards that were stationed surrounding them.

"We need more time," Prince Robert answered. Each word sounding like it took great effort for him to speak.

"Prince Robert," Lady Dori said.

She spoke so quietly that she had to repeat herself to be heard, "Prince Robert. I wonder if I might speak with you."

"Right now?" Prince Robert responded, trying not to sound annoyed.

"Perhaps we…" she began, her voice trailing off.

She looked down at the ground. Then, as if with renewed determination she looked straight into the young prince's eyes and said boldly, "Ask them to come again tomorrow. Tell them we will have a meal prepared for them and more to speak about at that time."

The princes looked to one another. Prince Samuel and Theodore both shrugged and Prince Robert looked back at the small woman standing before them appearing confident and determined.

He waited for a moment, gazing back at the restless crowd of Oblager.

"Very well then," he agreed with a sigh.

He turned toward the murmuring group of men at the back of the tent.

"Lord Silas," he spoke confidently to the elder man who had been identified by name earlier in the meeting.

"Just Silas," the man said. "No 'lord'."

Prince Robert nodded. "Silas, we would like to invite you to return tomorrow morning. We will have breakfast ready for you and more things to discuss."

"What could you possibly have to say that we would want to hear?" The more vocal, younger Oblager said.

"Erik!" Silas snapped, glaring at the young man who stood tall, hands on hips, as if daring anyone to challenge him.

The group's leader looked back at Prince Robert and tilted his head, almost politely, "We will accept your invitation for a meal. And then we will leave. I hardly think there will be anything worth discussing."

Without another word the group of men, all strong from the work of sailing and skin tan from the sun, left the tent and walked back down the cliffs toward their ships.

Throughout the entire meeting the Doyen had not said a word. But Sir Edward stepped forward now and whispered to the princes, "We could demand they leave these shores tonight, go down to the docks in full-force and tell them they cannot stay."

Or we could sink their ships in the night and be done with it, Prince Theodore thought. He wouldn't dare say it aloud, but he did think it and was ashamed of himself.

After watching all of the men disappear onto their ships the princes, their Doyen, the guards and Lady Dori all gathered around the meeting table.

Lady Dori and Prince Robert stood at the back of the tent and only their whispers could be heard. Lady Dori was unrolling a scroll to show Prince Robert.

"Your Grace, this is a map of the Island of Drepos. It has been in my family for centuries. You and your parents visited it every summer until your mother died. Do you remember it?" Lady Dori asked, eyes fixed intently upon her prince.

Prince Robert looked at the map and nodded slowly. "I do remember. Drepos is the Garden Island."

Lady Dori's smile spread across her face, "Yes, that is right."

"I know that this land is the only privately owned land in my father's, in my kingdom," Prince Robert said. "But how will that help us now?"

"The Oblager remember, as well as we do, their attack on this land when your ancestor High King Augustavo was on the throne. They nearly conquered us then and would have if it were not for the alliance between the Cheval and our people."

"Yes, that is all part of our history, but what does the Isle of Drepos have to do with peace-keeping?"

"Prince Robert, I wish to offer you this land, the Isle of Drepos, to give to the Oblager."

When her prince did not speak and tilted his head in confusion Lady Dori continued, "They have no home, Your Grace. Perhaps they would be glad to accept the gift of one?"

Prince Robert's jaw dropped open as he realized for the first time what this noblewoman was suggesting.

"Give them a home," he said.

She smiled up at him and nodded, "Yes, that is right!"

She bowed her head and offered up the map, now rolled tightly and bound again with twine.

Prince Robert took the parchment in his hand and touched her shoulder gently.

"My lady, I do believe you are one of the wisest women I have ever known."

Lady Dori blushed and bowed lower. But the smile on her face could not be hidden.

The two returned to the table to inform the group of their plan.

CHAPTER EIGHT

Castle Grange was quieter than Prince William could remember it ever being. He kept up his duties at the dovecote, watching for any messages that might arrive at the castle. He received the confirmation that blacksmiths were assembled and beginning their work at the armory, a fact that he assumed his brothers would already be aware of since they were meeting very near to where the armory was located. He did not see much of his sisters as they were often out on the hill near Colline working on their house project.

William did notice however that Lady Susan and Lady Claire were behaving as if they were preparing for war. The history of the Oblager was not spoken of often, though there was a lot of lore around their culture. William knew the Oblager to be ruthless in the lands that they conquered. The clan would take whatever the land held that they were in need of to survive, leaving the land barren.

The young prince could tell by the way Lady Susan and Lady Claire were storing up food, clothing and whatever tools might be necessary for life away from the castle that they were preparing for something. It seemed that they did not trust the peace negotiations to benefit the kingdom of Monde at all. Even Lord Nelson was behaving rather skittishly. Lord Nelson, who was usually mild-mannered and caught up in his work in the gardens, could be seen meeting with Lady Susan and Lady Claire to discuss preparations should the castle be "attacked". They had used that word. Prince William wondered what his role would be should the worst happen and they were attacked here at home. He felt a strong sense of duty to protect his sisters but he had not received much training in combat at his age. A young prince of Monde was taught to hold and wield weapons from the time he was old enough to stand. Combat training, however, was a different story. That training would come much later, just before he became a man, just before his thirteenth birthday. William was not yet of age to have received that type of training. He remained uncertain as to what he would or *could* do should the Oblager come to their gates.

"I'll do what I must," William said to himself out loud puffing his chest up, lifting his head higher, arms swinging wide as he walked. "I will protect my sisters and my home."

Speaking in this way did make him feel more confident as though he would indeed protect his sisters and his castle if it came to it, but he still had no idea as to how it would be done.

The next day the sun rose bright orange over the Beaumere Sea. The delegation representing the Kingdom of Monde was already assembled near the tent of meeting. Soon carriages from the castle would arrive bringing biscuits, honey, berries and goat's milk and cheese to share with the Oblager.

Prince Samuel was pacing outside the tent. He kept looking down the road hoping to catch sight of the group coming from the castle. He wanted to ride back to the castle with them but knew his place was here, in the tent, in the middle of talks with the Oblager.

Endurance stood nearby watching his young man pace. Samuel had seemed restless for some time but Endurance knew there was nothing he could do for his young man. Not yet, at least. Their path was not yet laid before them. Samuel was looking for something to do, waiting for something to happen and Endurance could sense it.

"They will be here soon, my young man," Endurance said to Samuel, drawing closer to him. "I sense your desire to go-"

"I know you will say it is not our time," Samuel cut in without looking at his blonde Cheval, "that I need to be here right now."

Then the young prince turned to look at Endurance, his brow furrowed with frustration. "I know this is my place but I feel useless."

"You are right," Endurance spoke softly, "your time, our time, will come sooner than we are aware. For now, we must continue to engage the Oblager and support Robert."

Samuel nodded his resignation. He walked toward the tent then broke into a run as he saw horse drawn carriages appearing in the distance.

"They're here," he yelled, still running toward them.

In moments Lady Claire, Lord Nelson and Princess Lillian were unloading the carriages from the castle.

"What in the heavens are **you** doing here?" Prince Samuel asked trying to remain calm at the sight of his sister.

He grabbed her by the arm and walked her back toward the carriages.

She looked down at his hand and groaned, "What are you doing?"

"You shouldn't be here," Samuel said. "It's too dangerous!"

"I'm helping with the meal," Lillian said. "What's dangerous about that? I can't continue to live in fear inside the castle walls. I must-"

"Lillian! What a surprise!" Robert interrupted.

"Robert, she shouldn't be here," Samuel urged his brother.

"True. This is not the safest place to be," Robert said. "But, she's here now… Let her do what she came for."

Samuel let out a sigh. Robert was right, she was here now, what could they do.

As the final bundles of food for breakfast were being brought into the tent the Oblager began to arrive.

Silas, was the first to enter the tent. He nodded respectfully to the princes before sitting down to the table with a couple of his men. Soon after him, Erik, the loud young man, arrived with a group of younger men. They spoke with Silas before taking their seats barely giving the princes a second glance. When Lillian came into the tent with a basket of biscuits Erik took notice.

"Who is this lovely creature?" Erik asked taking a biscuit out of the basket before Princess Lillian could even set it on the table.

Princess Lillian, tall and slender and gentle pulled her hand back too quickly causing her to drop the basket of biscuits onto the table.

Prince Samuel instinctively stood up putting his body between Erik and his sister.

Princess Lillian's pale cheeks turned pink and she kept her eyes low to avoid the heavy gaze of the stranger.

"She is our *younger* sister," Prince Samuel said in a controlled tone, emphasizing the word younger.

"Princess Lillian of the Kingdom of Monde," Prince Theodore added to stress her position and authority.

"One of the princesses," Erik smiled casually, popping part of a biscuit into his mouth and looking at Princess Lillian. "How good of you to join us."

Silas glared at Erik and with a hand gesture instructed him to sit back in his chair.

Prince Robert entered the tent in the midst of the exchange.

"She will be leaving now," he said calmly and escorted Princess Lillian from the tent to the carriages.

"Are you all right?" Robert asked a sister before helping her into the carriage.

"I'm fine," Lillian said, though her hands still shook as she grabbed the sides of her seat.

"I'll *be* fine," she corrected herself.

Robert squeezed the hand closest to him and kissed it.

"Go home where you'll be safe," he said.

She nodded in agreement.

Sir Nelson climbed up into the carriage beside the princess and looked over at Prince Robert with a reassuring glance.

"I'll get her home quickly and safely, Your Grace," he said.

Once Lady Claire was inside the carriage, Prince Robert let go of it and watched until it was safely on the road back toward the castle.

The morning got off to a slow start. The men from the ships seemed ravenous. Prince Theodore remarked to Samuel that it seemed the men hadn't eaten in days. They were still eating when finally Prince Robert cleared his throat for attention and began to speak.

"Thank you for coming back to speak with us today," Prince Robert began. "As promised, we have something we would like to discuss with you, something we hope will mark the start of peaceful relations between our house and yours."

"Relations?" Erik mumbled barely audible but just loud enough to be heard, "I'll marry that sister of yours in two or three years and that will give a good start to our *relations*."

Prince Samuel's eyes were wide as he looked to Robert to do or say something to Erik, to address the comment. But Prince Robert pretended he did not hear a thing. Instead, he turned to Silas and continued.

"I present to you Lady Dori."

The small woman came forward as she was being introduced and bowed her head slightly keeping her eyes low. Her guard, Elijah, took two steps forward as well.

"Lady Dori," Silas said with a slight nod. Then he turned to Prince Robert waiting for an explanation.

"Lady Dori has something she would like to offer you," Prince Robert explained further. "She does so with our blessing."

All of the men turned to look at the small gray-haired, gray-eyed woman standing at the center of the head table. When after a moment no word was spoken Erik began to chuckle quietly. Silas kept his eyes fixed on Lady Dori.

The woman's small shoulders rose then fell and she looked up from the ground straight into Silas's eyes.

"The Island of Drepos has been in my family for centuries. It is the garden island not 10 miles north-east of Falaise Bay. It is my birthright, my inheritance, but on behalf of the Kingdom of Monde, the House of Rosh, on behalf of my Prince Robert, I offer it to you and your people so that you can make a home of your own there."

There was a pause and it was the younger Oblager's turn to look astonished. He sat with his mouth gaping open, staring at the woman as she spoke.

Lady Dori continued, "Should you accept this land from me and my princes we wish you joy and peace as you make your home there."

Silas rubbed his face with one hand. He waited, choosing his words carefully. "Lady Dori, Prince Robert, Prince Theodore, Prince Samuel," he bowed his head to each one as he spoke their name, "we thank you for the offer."

Erik let out a loud sigh, as if he were bored, or perhaps annoyed.

Silas continued in a soft voice, "We thank you for the *offer*, but are unable to accept. We are a voyaging people. Our life is at sea; our home the rolling waves and the open sky. While this is a generous offer, it is not one we can accept."

"Kind Sir," Lady Dori said, "you have led your people and provided for them at sea for many lifetimes. Perhaps having a place to call home, a place *surrounded* by the rolling waves and open sky would lessen the burden of leading your people? Perhaps it would lessen the burden of the every day life for your people?"

At this Erik rose from his seat and pounded his clenched fists on the table.

"Who are *you* to tell us what would be best for *our* people?" He spat.

"Erik! Sit down," Silas instructed as calmly as he could, a slight blush rising in his cheeks.

"Are you going to let them speak to us in this way?" Erik asked Silas directly, still standing. "Like they would know what's best for *us*? "

"This is a peace offering," Silas said, each word pressured. "We will listen to what they have to say."

Erik looked at the group of men seated around him. They were all looking to him to see what he might do next. He turned back to Silas and said between clenched teeth, "you can sit here and listen to what they have to say but I will not."

Without another word Erik turned and left the tent. Ten men, maybe a dozen, stood and followed the young man out of the tent.

Silas took a moment to relax his clenched jaw and tightened fists. With a deep breath he turned to Prince Robert who was standing with his hand on Lady Dori's arm to support her in the heated exchange.

"Please accept my apologies, Prince Robert, Lady Dori. While this generous offer is most likely one we will not be able to accept, I wanted to show you the respect of listening to you. Young Erik has much to learn..."

Lady Dori inclined her head toward the man in acceptance of his apology. Prince Robert too nodded understanding.

Silas' shoulders seemed to slump and he sat back in his chair. "It seems there is nothing more that can be done today and so we thank you for our breakfast and will leave you now."

The remaining men seated nearest to Silas began to mumble and whisper to one another, gathering up remaining biscuits and fruit to take to the ships with them.

Lady Dori stepped forward and spoke calmly, "Please do consider accepting this gift, Silas. We offer you peace and a place to rest, a place to call your own."

He stood and nodded.

"A place to rest? We're not dead yet!" One of the men mumbled as he headed toward the back of the tent.

"Rest? A day on the beach, now that sounds good to me," another one said as the men began to descend the hill to the bay.

Prince Robert turned toward Lady Dori and smiled. "You handled that quite well," he said.

She smiled up at her prince.

"I was holding my breath half of the time, but we made it through, didn't we?"

Sir Logan stepped forward for the first time since the meeting began. He gave an approving pat to Elijah, the young shoulder he had commissioned to stay near Lady Dori.

"Their quarrel is among themselves," he said, "not with you. I was not worried today."

Lady Dori chuckled, "I'm so glad *you* were not worried, Sir Logan!"

CHAPTER NINE

Princess Margaret was waiting at the castle gate for the return of the carriages that had been sent to the port. She had been shocked both that her sister would have volunteered to go and that Lady Claire had let her. Lillian had been so concerned about the arrival of the Oblager just days before and then this morning she had thrown all caution aside to go feed them.

In moments the click-clack of horses hooves could be heard on the bridge and then entering the gate and before long Princess Lillian was telling her sister about everything she had seen and heard while at the port.

"How did it go?" Margaret asked her sister as she helped to unload the carriage.

"I don't know," Lillian said. "Perfectly fine... I think."

"Did you see any of them?" Margaret asked.

"Of course I did," Lillian shrugged as though laying eyes on a member of the Oblager people was an everyday occurrence.

"The nerve of that young man," Lady Claire began as she caught up to the girls walking toward the castle.

She was carrying her empty baskets back to the kitchen and must've moved quickly on her short legs in order to catch up to them.

"What young man?" Princess Margaret said, turning her head toward Lady Claire so quickly her dark curls bounced into her face.

She pulled the hair away and asked again, "What did you say? What young man?"

"There was a young man there who became far too familiar with your sister," Lady Claire explained. "It seems he is confident that he will soon be in a position of authority here."

Concern carved a line in Princess Margaret's forehead. "Do you think that's possible, Lady Claire? Really?"

"Oh, I wouldn't concern yourself," Lady Claire smiled warmly and tilted her head toward Princess Margaret, "I have complete faith in Lady Dori. If anyone can tame a beast, it's her. And with the Cheval, the Doyen and your brothers all working together, that's a force to be reckoned with."

Princess Lillian and Princess Margaret looped their arms around Lady Claire's reassuringly.

"I suppose you're right," Princess Margaret said at last, "They know what they're doing. All shall be well."

The princesses thanked the lady for her encouraging words and went to their rooms. Margaret knocked gently on Lillian's door shortly after they had separated.

"Come in."

Margaret stepped inside and closed the door gently behind her. The fire crackled in its hearth and cast golden light onto the bed across the room. Lillian was already in it and she peeked from beneath the covers.

"Can I sleep with you?" Margaret asked. "I think all that talk about the Oblager has made me a little … um … nervous."

"Come here," Lillian said.

"I was nervous too," she explained as her little sister crawled in bed beside her. "I was nervous but when I saw them and saw that they're just people too, I wasn't so scared anymore. That and Sir Logan is most definitely stronger than any of the Oblager I saw there today!"

Margaret smiled, reassured by her sister's words.

"Now, let's think of something else, like William's upcoming birthday celebration!"

The two princesses shared ideas for decorations, cakes and gifts until they both drifted off to sleep.

That night the Cheval gathered with the princes, the guards, the Doyen and Lady Dori around the fire.

"We must discuss our strategy in the event the Oblager refuse to accept the gift we have offered them," Sir Logan began the difficult conversation.

It was a conversation no one wanted but everyone knew needed to be had.

"A sneak attack?" Prince Theodore said, or rather asked of all of his collaborators.

He looked around cautiously as he waited for a reaction to his proposal. No one spoke.

Finally, Sir Logan said, "I must admit I have thought of it. But I'm not certain that's the way to go. The Oblager are very fierce warriors. They are ferocious in battle, but not because of strategy, because of their tenacity and strength. Though, it may not be difficult to surprise them."

A few paces from the fire Ardor pounded a hoof into the ground restlessly.

"It seems that Silas is willing to have a conversation with us," the Sage Cheval spoke gently. "It is the younger Oblager, Erik, that seems to have a problem with the idea. I believe he has his own plans."

There were a few mumbles and nods from the others sitting around the fire.

The crickets could be heard chirping in the stillness of the night. The fire crackled and snapped as it consumed the branches it was fueled by. Evenings were becoming very cool now and the fire gave off much-needed heat.

Lady Dori leaned in closer to the fire and held out her hands to receive its warmth.

"I think we should take them there," she said.

Everyone looked at her.

Prince Samuel turned to look at her squarely.

"What do you mean? Take them to the *island*?"

The small woman nodded.

"Perhaps if they see the place they may be able to envision a peaceful life there."

"This makes sense," Sir Francis acknowledged. "If they are able to see what it is we are offering perhaps they will be more inclined to take it."

"And if the worst should happen and they attack while we are at sea," Sir Logan spoke with a level tone, "we could lead them to the shoal to the west of the Isle of Drepos and they would run their ships aground."

Again the air was filled with the sounds of night as everyone thought of Lady Dori's proposal.

Prince Robert stood very near to Ardor and moved to press his forehead to the horse, seeking peace and wisdom in his friend.

After some time Prince Robert stood and said, "It is a risk, taking the Oblager out to see the island. However, it very well may be worth the risk to show them all that they would gain from accepting our offer. We will pose it to them in the morning. But for now, let's get some rest."

As everyone headed to their tents for the evening Prince Robert pulled Sir Logan aside.

"Send one of your men to retrieve Malaya. I'm not sure the information we need will be gained by asking direct questions."

Sir Logan bowed and went to send out his soldier that would bring the spy back to camp.

CHAPTER TEN

It was time. Margaret felt they had waited long enough and had done enough work for the craftsman of the kingdom to be called to the sheep farm on the hill. So that morning Margaret, Lillian and William headed out to the cottage near Colline early. They wanted to arrive before the artisans from throughout the villages that would gather at the cottage to begin their work. Much to their surprise some of the men were already there working. Some were laying brick and others were removing more of the wood from the house, the wood that would be of no use to build on. Margaret couldn't contain her excitement.

William laughed out loud at his sister as they dismounted their Cheval and walked over to the working crew. Some of the men's wives had come as well and were setting up an area where the men could come for food or drink if they needed a break.

Princess Lillian was talking with some of the women while Prince William and Princess Margaret were drawn to the work being done on the house. The men worked mostly in silence and the scraping of the tools could be heard ringing on the crisp morning air.

Prince William was invited by one of the men to join him in laying brick. After a short while the young prince was laying brick on his own, without the aid of the craftsman. Princess Margaret had busied herself inside the house. She wanted to tidy it, to add furniture, to see it the way she had seen it not too long ago in her memories and in her dreams. She knew she have to be patient and wait for the to be done, but that was hard - waiting.

When Margaret walked back out into the full light of day she saw her older brother, her "twin" for another couple weeks anyway, hard at work laying brick into the broken down outer wall. She stopped and shielded her eyes from the sun that was now high over the trees. William saw her smiling up at him and stopped what he was doing, as if embarrassed by her attention.

"Don't stop!" Margaret yelled, "You look like you're enjoying yourself!"

"I am!" William admitted, returning to his work scraping the mud mixture on top of one brick and laying another firmly on top of that. "I prefer working with birds over bricks but this work does have a pleasant rhythm to it."

And indeed it did have a rhythm that even Margaret was enjoying. The "swoosh" of the tool spreading the mud mixture then the soft "thwack" sound of a brick being laid. Swoo-oosh … thwack … Swoo-oosh … thwack … and so on.

Soon Princess Lillian was calling to the workers to come and relax themselves in the shade with some food and drink. The men did not hesitate when called to lunch and Princess Margaret and Prince William followed close behind.

"This morning has gone so quickly!" William remarked to his sisters and his Cheval who was standing near them.

"Hard work often makes time speed along," Allegiance agreed with his young man. "And you did work hard this morning."

William smiled with a bite of cheese in his mouth.

"I'm happy to see the progress," Margaret said.

"And attempting to remain patient and steady as it goes," Delight added. "I can tell you are trying."

Margaret put her arm under the neck of her Cheval to hug the horse's head closer to her own. She was shining an apple on her dress and bit into it before saying, "I AM trying."

"Margaret!" Lillian scolded as her sister spoke with a mouth full of apple.

"William just-" Margaret began but was cut off by her sister.

"I'm talking about you and *your* manners!" Lillian sighed. "Anyway, you both need to chew with your mouths closed."

"Why are you so upset?" Margaret asked.

"Yeah, like you've never seen me talk with my mouth full before," William added.

Lillian rolled her eyes at her youngest brother and sighed again. She leaned on Temperance and stroked her side for comfort.

"I'm still trying to trust Robert and Lady Dori; to trust that the Oblager will soon be sailing away. It doesn't feel right, knowing that there are strangers in our land and Father isn't here to protect us."

Temperance nuzzled closer to her girl.

Margaret came closer and consciously chose not to take a bite of her apple before saying, "You know Robert and Lady Dori are doing the best that they can."

"Besides," William came closer too and put his hand near Lillian's on Temperance's side, "the armory is operational and the king's guard is back to full strength. We will be just fine."

Lillian gave a weak smile to her siblings and rested her head on Temperance.

"I would certainly like to believe that."

CHAPTER ELEVEN

Morning on the cliffs near Falaise Bay was dark, cloudy and cold. In the near distance the peaks of the Sommet Mountains were etched against the gray of the sky. They seemed to match the color of the day and the sky seemed to hang low. The cold wind was full of sea air as it whipped up the side of the cliff and swirled around the tents.

The early risers of the camp were quick to start the morning fires. As each person rose they first went to the fires to warm themselves then set off in search of food. There were biscuits and honey left over from the day before but all fresh fruits and berries had been consumed.

Prince Theodore greeted his twin beside the fire, taking a bite of an apple he had saved from the day before.

"Good morning," he said with a mouthful.

"Hm. *Perfect manners*," a female voice spoke sarcastically from behind the hungry prince.

Prince Theodore turned to see a cloaked figure coming toward the fire and from under the hood a pair of large gray-blue eyes could be seen.

The twin princes nodded a greeting, "Malaya, good to see you again," Prince Samuel said. "Have you had any breakfast yet?"

"It is good to see you again, as well, my prince. And yes, I have eaten, thank you."

She bowed low before Prince Samuel, rose, bowed slightly toward Prince Theodore and walked away from the fire to stand near Sir Logan and Prince Robert.

"What was that?" Prince Theodore asked, watching Malaya as she went. "You get a deep curtsy and I get a nod?"

"It might have something to do with your *manners*?" Prince Samuel suggested with a smile, letting the dimple in his left cheek show. He dodged to the side just as his brother lifted his leg to kick at him.

"Haha!" Prince Samuel laughed, "poor manners and poor aim! We are in trouble!"

Theodore dove at his brother with a grin on his face, but before he could get his arms around him, Samuel was running back towards the tent. Theodore followed at top speed.

Prince Robert smiled and watched his brothers run away then turned back to the conversation he was having with Malaya and Sir Logan.

"There may be another way," Sir Logan was saying.

Malaya tilted her head to show her interest.

Prince Robert looked down into the bay at the ships anchored there.

"Can you swim?" He asked the spy.

CHAPTER TWELVE

The Oblager came to the tent in the middle of the day. Though some time had passed since they had all sat together last, the anger that the men had shown in the tent the day before was still there, Prince Samuel could feel it as he entered the tent to find all of the Oblager seated at the table where they had been the day before, and the men at the back also in their positions.

Sir Logan, it seemed, had added to the number of guards at the front of the tent surrounding the young princes, the Doyen and Lady Dori.

The day was cool and the wind whipped mercilessly through the tent causing Lady Dori to shiver. She was determined to get the older Oblager, Silas, to agree to visit the island.

Today, she said to herself, *today is the day we see progress in these negotiations.*

From his place at the back of the tent the young Oblager, Erik, began to laugh.

"Here we all are," he said, "a bunch of fools."

His smile suddenly disappeared from his face and his brow furrowed forming a deep V in his forehead.

"What are we doing here, Silas?" he asked, stepping forward to look the older man in the eye. "We have nothing left to say!"

Silas stood to confront the young man eye to eye.

"We have discussed this," Silas said through clenched teeth. "Now *step back* and shut your mouth!"

The young man paused.

Prince Theodore stood slowly waiting for this argument to come to blows. He knew he was much younger and perhaps not as experienced as these men but also knew he would not run from a fight.

To everyone's surprise Erik shut his mouth. He looked as though he were chewing on his lips to keep them closed. Slowly, he moved back, step-by-step, keeping his eye on Silas. Finally he took his place by his men.

"Now," Silas said with a new tone of confidence, "we *have* discussed this and have decided we will see this island you want to give us."

Lady Dori looked at the man wide eyed. She had expected to have to do some more convincing before they would accept. She breathed a sigh of relief that today would be the day they would take the Oblager to see the island, her island, hopefully soon-to-be *their* island.

"Very good!" Prince Robert said hopefully, rising to his feet and clapping his hands together. "Please, Silas, let us take you and a dozen of your people to see the place. Lady Dori and I will take you, and my captain with a few of our guard will accompany us as well.

Silas briefly looked behind him at Erik then back at Prince Robert and nodded.

"Let us go to the docks now, there will be a ship there waiting to take us."

When Silas raised his eyebrows Prince Robert put his hand up.

"We wanted to be prepared in the event you accepted our invitation," he explained.

Again, without a word, Silas nodded and turned to leave the tent.

The Isle of Drepos could be seen from the docks at the port in Falaise Bay. It was eight nautical miles from the mainland, which could take over two hours to sail to.

Lady Dori hugged her shawl tighter around her. It would be a windy ride, but the wind was indeed a blessing for it held the potential to shorten their ride just a bit. The less time they would all spend together on a tiny ship, the better, she decided.

It was a quiet ride and much faster than any of them had anticipated. Erik and the men who usually gathered around him seemed unaffected by the beauty of the island as it came into view. Silas, however, seemed to try to keep his interest in check, hiding a smile behind a cupped hand and pretending to clear his throat.

The island was beautiful. There was a slight mountain at the center of it and the land was green with foliage. A thick layer of trees obstructed the path to the mountain but even in the midst of such a dense forest there were trails and a few clearings, which would be ideal for building.

Lady Dori took a deep breath of the sea air and looked all around her. She loved this island. She had been visiting it for as long as she could remember. The sandy shore was always soft and welcoming to her. It led to a gradual incline where grass grew green and tall. The grassy knoll eventually ran into large trees that grew all throughout the center of the island. The place was perfect for habitation but Lady Dori knew her family had never considered living here; their devotion and service had always been to the king and queen at Castle Grange. As such, it had been important to live on the mainland, to be close to the castle in case they were ever called upon by the royal couple, which had been often throughout the years. As her family had served, so Lady Dori had been at last called into the full-time service of Queen Amalia. Her life had changed forever then as a resident of Castle Grange. But her heart would always love this island.

Once the ship was safely moored the party disembarked, loaded onto the dock and then the shore. Lady Dori led the way. It was her island after all. As they entered the beach she turned to look back at the Oblager, her silver hair whipping her face. Silas and Erik were walking together, neither saying a word. Silas was looking all around him, seeming to take it all in. Lady Dori noticed that Erik, on the other hand, was staring straight ahead of him, a look of defiance on his face.

"Let's go further in," Lady Dori instructed, trying to speak over the sound of the wind and the waves.

Everyone followed.

CHAPTER THIRTEEN

Princess Margaret was used to being involved in things throughout the kingdom so the fact that the peace talks were happening at Falaise Bay and she was stuck back at the castle away from the action frustrated her. She had been nervous, afraid even, but her sister had been brave enough to face the Oblager.

"And if she was able to do it, I'm sure I could do it too," Princess Margaret said aloud to herself.

Even with thoughts almost constantly on the Oblager and their ships docked at the port, she had remained distracted by her plans for the house that Lillian had agreed to help her restore. That little brown house on the side of the hill near Colline had drawn her in at a very difficult time in her young life. She felt a longing to care for it now, to see it restored.

The help of the elder craftsman in the villages had proven to be invaluable. The younger men were already being organized to work in the armory at the foothills of the Sommet mountain range. And those who were not working in the armory were being trained for combat. Those who had come to help build the house, to spend their time and energy on it meant more to Margaret than she was able to put into words. They had all been so willing to be there even though it was a strange time for the Kingdom of Monde. It was a strange time for her as well, she decided. As long as she had been alive they had never been threatened by war. At least not that she knew of or could remember. Now here they were on the very edge of war and it felt… *strange.*

Princess Margaret went to the kitchen early in the morning, her head full of thoughts and her stomach empty. She knew if she went to the kitchen this early she would find Lady Claire there.

"Good morning, Princess," the lady said as she loaded a basket full of fresh biscuits.

Princess Margaret took a deep breath full of the savory smell of bread baking in the ovens. That never got old. And she would never tire of the flavor of Lady Claire's biscuits topped with the honey Lady Susan procured from the honeybees kept in the castle apiary.

"Are you hungry this morning?" Lady Claire asked.

"Yes, I am hungry, Lady Claire," Princess Margaret said with a smile taking a biscuit from the basket. It was still warm. She pressed it to her lips as if kissing it and inhaled deeply once again before opening her mouth to take a bite.

"Lady Claire," Princess Margaret asked after a couple bites, "has the Kingdom of Monde ever been at war? In recent history, I mean."

Lady Claire wiped her hands on her apron and walked over to Princess Margaret. She invited the young princess to sit on the stool next to her.

"Well," Lady Claire spoke softly and slowly as if carefully choosing her words. "Most recently, the kingdom has not seen war. But that is not to say that we have not had an occasion nor the need to defend ourselves."

Princess Margaret swallowed the last of her biscuit with the gulp.

"What do you mean?"

"We have been threatened before. Since I have been here at the castle. Since your father has been king."

"Well, how did it happen?" Princess Margaret asked with eyes wide.

"There were unknown ships in the Beaumere Sea for days," Lady Claire explained. "We were just watching them, unsure as to whether or not they planned to enter the bay. Quite like when the ships of the Oblager showed up out of nowhere. But, back then, we watched, unsure as to whether or not they were friend or foe."

"Did we have many ships at that time?" Princess Margaret asked. "It seems like we barely have any ships now."

"We did have quite a few ships then. Perhaps twice what we have now since your father took the rest to Estrella with him…"

Lady Claire's voice trailed off and both she and Princess Margaret seemed to be staring at the same spot on the floor. Princess Margaret couldn't help it but she felt tears stinging her eyes. She sniffled away the tears and the lonely thoughts of missing her father, raised her chin and asked, "What happened then?"

Lady Claire followed the lead of her young princess and lifted her head as well. "It all came to nothing. We sailed out to meet them, armed to the teeth and when they saw we would not be an easy conquest the ships sailed away."

"Lady Claire, what do you think we will do now?" Princess Margaret asked staring directly into the deep brown eyes of her kind lady.

"Just like your father, if it comes to it, we will meet them at sea, of course."

CHAPTER FOURTEEN

Night had fallen on the coast of the Kingdom of Monde. The sailing party had returned from the island long enough for a meal to be eaten and most of the group had already returned to their tents. Princes Theodore and Samuel sat by the fire talking to the Doyen about the day they had had.

"Lady Dori was amazing," Prince Samuel said.

The group agreed and Sir Francis leaned forward and poked the fire with a stick to stir it up. In the distance Prince Robert was spending some time in prierie with Ardor. It had been quite some time since the two of them had enjoyed these moments of peace and quiet together.

Prince Robert stood with his forehead pressed against Ardor's muzzle. His hands held the strong jaw of his Cheval. In the distance Prince Robert heard shuffling noises and a guard saying, "Who goes there?"

Both Ardor and the prince looked up into the darkness.

"I'll go," Prince Robert said and headed into the darkness toward the voices. When he reached the edge of the camp he was surprised to see Silas and a couple of his seafaring men being held back by the night watchmen.

"What's happening here?" Prince Robert asked.

Then he looked at Silas with a sideways glance and asked, "Sir, may I ask what you're doing here?"

Silas looked directly at Prince Robert and clenched his jaw. The older man was not tall but was very solid and he struggled against the pressure put on his arm by the guard.

"I need to speak with you," he said staring directly into the eyes of the Acting King of Monde.

Prince Robert inclined his head toward them and the guards released Silas and his men. Silas took one cautious step forward and got as near to Prince Robert as he dared and whispered his thanks. But that wasn't all.

"I *need* to speak with you." His voice was soft but urgent.

Prince Robert could hear the rasp in the man's voice; a voice filled with emotion not malice, and the prince knew the man was in earnest.

"What have you come to tell me?" Prince Robert asked.

The man looked again at his men and back at Prince Robert.

"May we sit and talk?"

Sir Logan, Captain of the Guard, took one step toward the men as if in warning. Prince Robert again looked the man hard in the face. He could tell that the man was not here to create mischief. There was something deep in the Silas's eyes and Robert was trying to make out what he saw there. Was it desperation? Was it longing? The prince held out his hands to motion toward the nearest fire.

Prince Robert, Silas and his men all sat around the fire. The guards stood close behind Prince Robert. Within moments their group was joined by Prince Theodore and Sir Edward, both with bewildered looks on their faces. They sat near to Prince Robert at the fire and when everyone was settled Silas spoke.

"Prince Robert," Silas leaned forward putting his forearms on his left knees and again looking intently at the young prince.

"We would like to accept your offer. We would like to accept the gift of the Isle of Drepos to be our home."

Prince Robert felt his shoulders relax. He let out a sigh and realized he had been holding his breath.

"I'm very happy to hear it, Silas. But why come to us in the dark of night to bring us this news?"

"I wanted to talk to you privately before accepting your offer publicly..." His voice trailed off.

He looked from side to side, then to his men, then at the prince.

"I'm afraid there are some of my people who do not agree with this. I'm concerned as to what they may do should I accept. But I will tell you this, as for me and my house, we are willing to pledge our friendship and loyalty to the house of Rosh and to live at peace with you and all of the Kingdom of Monde."

After a time of silence with Silas staring into the flames as if searching for something there, he looked up again and said, "I am tired. I am weary of living restless lives, my people and I. It is time to begin a new life. It is time to make our own way and to live at peace."

Prince Robert waited a moment before speaking. He looked to Sir Edward and to his brother. They both had their eyes on him as if waiting to hear what he might say.

"If what you say is true," Prince Robert said, "and you desire to live in friendship with my people, then my family will help you to make the Isle of Drepos your home. We will help you, no matter what some of your people might say to you."

Prince Theodore shot up straight in his seat and stared at his brother. Prince Robert held up a hand to steady him. Sir Edward's eyebrows were raised but he said nothing. Sir Logan and the guard stood behind the prince and clicked their heels together as if to stand a little straighter, at the ready.

This time it was Silas who exhaled audibly. And he seemed to relax as well. A slight smile was forming at the edges of his mouth when he looked up once again.

"I am relieved to hear you say it," he said. "I will be honest with you, I believe Erik may be planning to rise up against me. But I cannot say how or when. In our meeting tomorrow I will publicly accept your gracious offer of a home for my people. And I cannot tell you how light it makes my heart feel to know that we are indeed welcome here."

Prince Robert could not contain his smile. He stood and walked to Silas and held out his hand. The man shook it firmly accepting the handshake and bowing his head to the Acting King of Monde.

Silas and his men left to return to their ship. Prince Theodore still sat upright in his chair, a look of shock on his face.

"Did. That. Just. Happen?" He had to ask.

"Why yes," Prince Robert reassured him. "It is a good thing, brother. We are forming an alliance, and a mighty one at that."

Prince Theodore stood and walked toward his brother as he spoke, "We are making friends with an old man who cannot defend himself against those of his *own people* who would rebel against him."

"We are forming an alliance with a mighty people. They are strong and they are skilled at sea," Prince Robert countered. "That is something we lack."

"Yes, skilled at sea," Prince Theodore responded, "and we are asking them to come and sit on our island. How strong do you think they'll be when their lifestyle changes to one of land dwellers? Not to mention the fact that we have no idea how many people Erik will draw to him in rebellion of Silas and this move to the Isle of Drepos. What if it is all of their elders who wish to live on the island and we're fighting a war with the younger Oblager? We would be fighting those who are the strongest and who are fearless and relentless to preserve the way of life they've always known. No, brother, this is not a good thing, this is madness."

Prince Robert stood with his hands on his hips. He was breathing heavily but had no words to say. The fire cracked in the midst of the silence. The insects of the night could be heard chirping and croaking their songs. And still the young men stood face-to-face, not one speaking. Finally, Sir Edward stepped forward and cleared his throat to break the silence.

"If I might, my princes," he said, "this indeed is a risky proposition."

Prince Theodore looked up in agreement, "Yes, it is!"

Sir Edward put his hands up and said, "and yet, it may be very much worthwhile to pursue."

Prince Robert looked up at the man and smiled, "yes, I do believe it *will be* worthwhile."

CHAPTER FIFTEEN

Princess Lillian found it very satisfying to watch the craftsman at work. She thought it was amazing the way that they could take the wood, hammer and nail to create something as beautiful as an entryway to the sweet brown cottage on the hillside near Colline.

Princess Margaret was very excited as she watched her dream of the house being restored come to life. She was thrilled as the bricklayers restored the walls of the home. She was even invited to help lay a brick or two throughout the day while Prince William instructed her. He had been working diligently with the bricklayers and had become quite adept at the craft.

The youngest royal children found the work of the day to be a welcome distraction. They helped the artisans in whatever way possible and kept themselves very busy.

"What are we going to do with this house once it's complete?" William asked his sisters.

They were taking a break under the shade of a tree with their Cheval.

"Well, I have a million ideas about that and just haven't been able to land on one," Margaret admitted, taking a sip of her water and a step closer to Delight.

"I'm still thinking that once it is restored that perhaps the youngest Lord Riley would like to reclaim if for his family," Margaret said.

"That is a lovely idea," Lillian said. "Let's have a ceremony to present it to him after the Oblager are gone. We can plan it together!"

Margaret smiled at her sister.

Ceremonies and celebrations were more of what Margaret enjoyed so she knew the suggestion had been made with her in mind. Lillian herself imaged bringing Lord Riley to the house on a quiet afternoon, just him and his family. But, since this project was Margaret's to begin with, the final say on how it would be awarded would be hers.

The rest of the day was very productive at the house and except for finishing touches and personalizing the place, it was done. The three siblings went back to the castle that evening talking incessantly about what they liked best about the fully restored cottage.

"We'd love to ride out with you and see the house," Lady Susan said as she helped bring the meal into the dining room that evening.

"Yes, very much so!" Lady Claire chimed in from close behind.

"Well, at first I wanted to make you all wait until we were *completely* finished setting it up," Princess Margaret said. "But we're very close and I'm so excited I can't stand it! You should come and see the progress!"

The ladies laughed and agreed to go with their charges to the home the next day.

As evening fell the princesses returned to their rooms and Prince William made one last trip to the dovecote to check for messages. When he entered the round stone building he saw a single dove sitting on the perch at the center of the place. This was where doves were trained to return to when carrying a message. This little dove was indeed carrying a message. Prince William hurried to the pedestal and removed the scroll from the bird's leg, throwing down a handful of seed on the stand for the bird to eat. He unwrapped the message, read it and then ran back to the castle to share it with his sisters.

He found the girls in Lillian's room near the fire. The evenings were getting much colder and fires were being lit every night and every morning now. He ran over to them and showed them the tiny piece of parchment.

"This was waiting for me at the dovecote," he said.

Lillian snatched the paper from his hand and read it aloud, "Peace from your friends in the Kingdom of Allia. We send word to inform you that there are seven ships in the sea very near to our shores heading north toward the Kingdom of Monde. Be warned of their presence. Respectfully, King Facile of Allia."

"Well, that's old news," Margaret said.

William and Lillian seemed to remain on edge despite the fact that the sighting of the Oblager ships was indeed old news.

William looked at Lillian and said, "How many ships did you see in the port?" Lillian shook her head "I... I... I don't remember."

"Why is that important?" Margaret asked. "I don't understand."

"What if this is a trap?" William asked. "What if they only brought some of their ships into the port while the others are off hiding in wait, ready to attack when the time is right?" William suggested.

"Well, I hadn't about *that*!" Margaret said getting up from her place by the fire. "We need to do something!"

Lillian grabbed her sister's hand and pulled her back down onto the rug beside her.

"There's nothing we can do in the middle of the night. First thing in the morning I'll take one of the guards and go back to the port to talk to Robert."

"Why you?" William shot a look at his older sister.

"Because I'm the oldest. And I've already been there once. In fact," Lillian stood and threw a cloak over her shoulders, "I'm going to talk with Temperance about this right now."

William and Margaret followed close behind.

Margaret grabbed a blanket to throw over her shoulders and said, "And I should talk to Delight about it too!"

"And Allegiance needs to know!" William added.

Lillian rolled her eyes and marched with purpose through the castle, out into the courtyard and toward the stables.

CHAPTER SIXTEEN

Prince Robert stood holding a mug of steaming hot water and honey in his hands. He held the drink up to his face and felt the warmth of the steam on his mouth and nose. It was a cool, breezy morning and looking down at the bay Robert watched the ships rocking and pitching in the waves. The whitecaps rolled into the bay and in the distance the Beaumere Sea was churning. He took a sip of his drink and looked again at the ships moored at the port.

Today is the day, he thought to himself. *Today we shall see what comes next.*

Where he had felt relief and even joy the night before, with the morning he felt only nervous and a nagging sense of dread. Robert held out one of his hands flat in front of him and watched it. It wasn't shaking. He took a moment to check in with every part of his body. He was well acquainted with anxiety and knew where he held his tension. But there was no evidence of fear in any of the usual places. No headache. No stomach cramps. No tension or shaking. He was strangely calm.

He had been so glad to hear Silas say that he was willing to accept the gift of the Isle of Drepos; so relieved to hear that Silas wanted to take his people in a new direction and to live at peace and harmony with the Kingdom of Monde. But thoughts of Erik and his agitated demeanor made Robert nervous this morning. Would the young Oblager conform? Would he comply and learn to live a new kind of life on Drepos or would he fight to the bitter end in order to preserve the way of life he had always known?

Prince Robert took another drink of the hot liquid. They would soon find out. Below him men were pouring onto the docks and walking toward the hill that would eventually lead them to the tent.

"Are you ready for this?" Theodore asked quietly, joining his brother at the ledge.

Robert turned around to look at him.

"As ready as I can be," he said. "And you?"

Theodore nodded.

In a moment the brothers they turned their backs to the group of men climbing the side of the hill and walked back to the tent together to try to prepare for whatever would come next.

Princes Robert, Theodore and Samuel were already seated at the table. Lady Dori and Sir Logan were standing behind them. They could hear the men were already negotiating amongst themselves before they entered the tent.

"It makes no sense to settle in one place."

"It is not *our way*."

"Well, I for one would like a place to call home!"

"The sea *is* our home!"

As the men entered the tent they halted their conversations. Hot drinks were brought in along with baskets full of biscuits that were starting to harden but still soft enough to be eaten. Lady Dori took the tiniest bites as she watched the men find their places inside the tent. The young men all stood at the back, as usual, as if they were ready to run for it if the need arose. The older men sat forward at the table, not just because they were the leaders, but also because they wanted to be nearest the princes and Lady Dori, nearest to the conversation.

Elijah, the young guard assigned to Lady Dori took a protective step closer to her as he had done the first day they had met the Oblager. She looked up at the man and smiled. The young man nodded and then snapped back to attention in an instant.

When everyone had a drink and biscuit in hand Prince Robert welcomed them as if he had not heard a word they had spoken upon their arrival.

"We hope to come to an understanding today," Prince Robert said, lifting his mug to the group. "We hope that we can agree to peace."

The prince drank from his mug.

Some of the men drank to the toast but Erik and many of the men nearest to him did not raise their mugs in agreement.

"There will *not* be an agreement," Erik said. "You want us to stay and be friendly, we want to take what we need and go. I see no middle ground."

"Were you able to see everything you wanted to see on the island when you were there?" Lady Dori asked. "It may take some time to get used to it and make it your own."

"I don't need a good look at it, the sea is mine and land only serves a purpose for a time."

Erik took a few steps back but continued to pace, his hands on his hips, shaking his head silently.

"And what about the Cheval?" He blurted out suddenly, stopping in his tracks and looking up at Prince Robert. "I see you've been keeping them separate from this meeting. Or have you been keeping them away from us? If we agree to all that you propose would you give us some Cheval of our own to make our lives easier?"

Prince Robert stepped forward and said, "We do not *own nor do we rule* the Cheval. We live in relationship with them, we partner with them. We do not dictate to them. They are not ours to sell or give away."

Prince Robert was standing now, his cheeks red with anger.

Lady Dori stepped forward and said quietly, "We have offered you what is ours to give. The Cheval have free will. The mainland of the Kingdom of Monde is a peaceful land. The Isle of Drepos will be yours to keep, should you choose to accept it. My gracious prince has told you we could live at peace near one another and yet you choose to continue to argue and to push for more. The question now, young Sir Erik is this: will *you* accept the gift given you or will you refuse it?"

No one spoke. Time seemed to stand still. The wind howled its way through the flaps of the tent then stopped. Silence.

"Why not winter on the island and see how you like it?" Prince Samuel suggested when the silence lasted too long for his comfort. "You may change your mind."

Erik's laugh was exaggerated in response to this suggestion and he shook his head, walking toward the front of the tent to stand next to the place where Silas sat.

"I will *never* change my mind!" He said this more to Silas than to the prince.

Silas rose to his feet.

"Step back, Erik, and watch yourself! The final decision is mine."

The young man shook his head, a look of disgust on his face as he stepped back from the table and looked around the tent, his gaze finally resting on Silas.

"I blame *you* for this," he said. "*You*'re the one who accepted the invitation to talk to them in the first place. Now you want to accept the gift of *land*? You want to change our people's lives. Who are you to do so? You do not deserve to lead the Oblager!"

Silas was standing now too.

Sir Logan had doubled the amount of guards at the tent and they all stood ready for action should Prince Robert give the signal.

"I am the chief of the Oblager," Silas said with more anger than he had shown the entire few days of meetings. "I am the elder here and you, Erik, have little say in the matter. If our people have spoken and if I have declared it to be, it shall be so!"

Erik stood with his mouth open, staring at the elder Oblager, a fire burning in his eyes. When Silas was done speaking Erik turned and lumbered toward the back of the tent.

"We will not allow this, old man. We will not stand here and let you change *everything*!" With these last words Erik ran out of the tent and down the trail on the side of the hill toward the ships. A dozen men followed close behind.

Silas jerked to attention, realizing they were heading to the ships.

"Men!" He shouted to those who remained. "Go!"

His men needed no more instruction than this as they all chased after the younger men who already had a good head start back to the ships.

"I will handle this," Silas said, looking Prince Robert in the eye. "I will take care of Erik and we will live on the Isle of Drepos, at peace with the Kingdom of Monde."

Prince Robert nodded. "That is good to hear, Silas."

Silas reached out a hand and Prince Robert took it. Silas bowed down, kissed Prince Robert's hand then rose and fled from the tent.

Sir Logan was at Prince Robert's side.

"We will hold our ground and see how this plays out," Prince Robert instructed. "Sir Logan, dispatch a guard to the training yard and call up the men."

Sir Logan nodded and hurried to find a man to send.

"Theodore, I need you to go to the armory and have the men there send all weapons and armor that may be ready for use and bring them back."

Prince Theodore bowed, turned to find Honor close to the tent and soon the two disappeared into the morning mist.

"Samuel, I need you at the inn. Malaya will meet you there. She will have a report to give."

Prince Samuel nodded his head in understanding, hugged his brother then ran down the side of the hill and off to the south of the trail. He didn't want to get tangled up in the two separate groups of Oblager who were hurrying down the same hill toward their ships.

Prince Robert watched them all leave then choked on his breath. He put a calming hand to his chest and took a drink of water handed to him by Sir Logan. "You have this well in hand, my prince," the Captain of the Guard said. "And we are all with you."

Prince Robert stood tall, straightened his clothing and put a firm hand on Sir Logan's shoulder.

"And I shall need all of you," he said.

CHAPTER SEVENTEEN

The dining room at the back of the inn was dimly lit but there was a warm fire burning in the fireplace and Samuel went to stand near it and warm his hands. The sea air that was blowing in cold and damp from the bay had chilled him and he shivered as the warmth of the fire melted that chill away. It was midmorning and if the sun had been shining it may have burned away the mist that covered the little town at the port. Since it was overcast and dark this made it difficult to tell the time by the sun and almost impossible to get warm.

Samuel looked around the dark room. The place was empty. It was as if there were no ships moored right outside the doors and down past the docks. No men here to eat breakfast and no spy. Where was Malaya?

The prince started to fidget and pace in front of the fireplace. He didn't want to move too far from the heat it offered. A maid came out of the kitchen and began wiping down all the tables in preparation for the day. She kept looking up at the prince then bowing her head again shyly. He nodded to acknowledge her but tried not to make eye contact. For some reason he felt uneasy and so he paced back and forth. He took a moment to look out the window toward the docks and then returned to his pacing.

Finally, the maid left and again he was alone in the room. In a rush of wind and rain, the front doors of the place opened wide and the cool, moist air of the bay was released into the room. A hooded figure entered the inn, silently closed the doors and walked directly toward him.

A slim arm slid from beneath the cloak and the hood was lowered as the young woman curtsied slightly before Prince Samuel. Without waiting for him to respond or say a word she slipped her arm around his and led him out of the room through a door beside the fireplace. He hadn't even noticed the door before and looked at her in surprise. She guided him into the room and closed the door behind them. The room was small and dank with no windows to lend it light. Prince Samuel felt like he was in a box and he noticed the closeness made the air inside seem difficult to breath.

Malaya lit the candle that was on the small table. The table was one of the only things that the room held, other than two chairs and a couple of dirty mugs the maid must have missed.

"It wasn't safe out there in the open. When we are done here I will leave under cover and you will count to one hundred before you leave."

Prince Samuel nodded his consent and drew one of the chairs up to the table to be near the light.

"And, my prince, I can see you don't like this room, but you must count to one hundred by ones," she said this last part with a half smile and it made the young prince chuckle.

"Yes, ma'am," he replied, feeling a little more at ease.

He hadn't forgotten why they were here and neither had the young spy.

Malaya met her prince at the table.

"Have you discovered a way aboard the Oblager ships *without* having to swim it?" Prince Samuel asked with a smile.

She shook her head. "But I manage."

Prince Samuel nodded and the smile left his face.

"What is it like aboard?"

She spoke softly but urgently, "It is *chaos* on those ships. The young Oblager Erik has not said it within my earshot but I know he is planning something. He whispers and meets in secret with a dozen of the other men."

"We know that Erik and the clan leader Silas do not see eye-to-eye. They have fought in our presence. But what *could* Erik do? Has there been any word or do you have any sense of what his next move might be?"

Malaya shook her head. "But, I do know that whatever they choose to do Erik and his men have little to lose."

"What do you mean by that?"

"Their families, if they have any, are safely elsewhere. And, my prince-" Malaya stopped and leaned in closer, "I was able to find that they have another ship docked away from here and if there's one hidden ship there could be more. They may be planning an attack by sea."

Prince Samuel sat up straight. "Another ship! That *is* news! Thank you for your service, Malaya. Please stay safe."

She nodded and quickly pulled the heavy hood back up over her head, her face covered in shadows. She stood, touched Prince Samuel's arm and walked to the door. Before leaving through it she whispered, "One hundred!"

As soon as the door shut behind her the prince started counting to one hundred by ones. He tried not to count too quickly but felt even more anxious in the room now that he was alone. Once he reached one hundred he stood, blew out the candle on the table and felt for the door handle. The outer dining area was still empty, which he found a bit strange before realizing it wasn't quite lunchtime yet.

He was relieved when he was finally out into the fresh air that was blowing in off the Beaumere Sea. It was still cold and damp despite the fact that the sun had found its way through the clouds but Samuel didn't mind. He just wanted - no needed to get back to camp to tell Robert all he had learned.

By the time Samuel had trekked up the hill back into camp he found the men there were already preparing for the midday meal. Fires were lit throughout and food was already cooking. Samuel could smell it. He looked for Robert and found him very quickly near the tent of meeting. The prince was talking with the Doyen, Sir Logan and Lady Dori.

When they saw Prince Samuel walking toward them they made room for him around the fire and waited eagerly for him to speak.

"Erik has been meeting secretly with a group of men and Malaya said she has not been able to determine what it is they are planning, but it does not appear they will be joining the elder Oblager on the Isle of Drepos under any circumstance."

Everyone nodded in understanding.

Prince Samuel continued, "The most disturbing news, however, is that Erik and his men do not have their families with them here."

"I had always assumed the ladies and children were on the ships," Lady Dori said quietly, as if talking to herself.

Sir Logan sat upright, "That is the move of someone who plans to attack!"

Prince Samuel nodded, "Malaya thought as much. But the other concern is the ship they have left behind in reserve."

Prince Robert looked to Sir Logan just to be sure he was thinking correctly.

"Back up?" He suggested.

"That is what I would guess," Sir Logan confirmed.

Lady Dori said nothing but put her head in her hands.

"But back up for whom?" Prince Samuel asked the group. "If for Silas then all is well. But if Erik intends to attack our shores and the ship is loyal to him then-"

Sir Edward cut it in, "Wait. Any attack at sea is a problem for us. We are weakest at sea. What form of defense could we plan or what attack could we make from land, Sir Logan?"

"I will be able to outline all of our options when I know every resource available to us by land or sea."

Prince Robert stood. "We should all eat and get some sleep. We will meet at first light tomorrow in the tent. Prince Theodore should be returning soon from the armory. Let us hope he has plenty of weapons to offer us."

CHAPTER EIGHTEEN

Early that morning at the castle Princess Lillian dressed with an extra cloak over her shoulders for warmth. The morning was still dark with barely a hint of orange from the sun on the horizon after a long autumn night. Lillian was sure to pick up the message from Allia before leaving her rooms. She folded it carefully and slid it into the pocket of her dress then headed out to the stables.

Lillian was uncertain about how Temperance might take to the idea of riding out to Falaise Bay in the light of a new day. Their talk the night before had been brief and she and her siblings had not taken the time to listen to their Cheval after sharing the news of the message from Allia. Now that she would return more determined than the night before to head back to the port she was unsure about the response she would receive from Temperance. She had prepared a speech to give to her Cheval should the need arise, but before she had reached the stable she found herself headed off by Lady Susan and Lord Nelson. With few words they asked the princess to return to the castle immediately.

"My lord, my lady," she said as calmly as she could, "I have a message I must take to Prince Robert and I will thank you to step aside and allow me to do my duty."

"Princess," Lord Nelson begged, his hands clasped tightly together in front of his chest as if in prayer, "We would not be doing our duty to your father if we did not try to stop you. Please let someone else go. We don't know what is happening at the port and do not wish for you to be put into harm's way."

"You are welcome to ride with me," Princess Lillian said.

She had directed this last comment to Lady Susan for it was well known that Lady Susan was one of the most skilled riders in the kingdom.

Without a word Lady Susan bowed her head, went into the stables and was soon back out into the cool air of the morning with Solicitude by her side. The speckled mare stood tall and at the ready, waiting as Princess Lillian prepared Temperance for the ride to Falaise Bay.

Prince William ran out into the courtyard just in time to see the two Cheval and their companions turn their backs to the castle and trot toward the gates.

He stood next to Sir Nelson who had a furrow in his brow. The man kept moaning or humming, William wasn't sure which.

"Sir Nelson?" The young prince looked with concern at the older man.

"I'm quite alright, my prince," he said. "I am just concerned for us all. Is there any good that can come from this business at the port?"

"Prince Robert is confident and Lady Dori is a strong communicator. I want to believe we can have hope for some kind of resolution to all of this."

Sir Nelson turned to look at his young prince and with a tear in his eye he said, "I do hope that you and Prince Robert are right to hope and that those men will listen to Lady Dori and the peace that is being offered."

Sir Nelson walked away as if in slow motion toward the gardens.

Prince William sighed and shook his head.

Am I wrong to be so confident? He wondered to himself.

The wind began to blow with some force across the courtyard and once the gates were closed William returned to the castle to find Margaret.

The road wound its way through the forest, up and over hills and down into valleys, past Valea and across the plains. A small part of Colline could be seen up on the hillside with tufts of smoke rising from the fires that were now common in the mornings as fall quickly approached.

Once Colline was out of sight and the mountain road toward Ploin was behind them the lower road opened up to a glimmering horizon. The sun's rays that broke their way through the cloudy sky sparkled like diamonds across the Beaumere Sea, once there and then gone again as the clouds moved on.

Princess Lillian loved the water. It was so beautiful. It reminded her of the birthday rides she and her siblings would take out to the waterfalls that fell from the Sommet Mountain range.

"Princess," Lady Susan said and pointed to the small collection of tents on the hill above Falaise Bay.

"We're here," Princess Lillian confirmed and put a gentle hand on Temperance's neck. "Shall we?"

Temperance picked up her pace and Solicitude followed close behind.

As they neared the encampment the riders could see a flurry of activity in and around the tents. The hum of conversation could be heard amidst the flapping of the canvas tents as they snapped against the force of the wind.

"Lillian! What are you *doing* here?" Prince Robert said running to her side and helping her out of the saddle.

He hugged her then pushed her away from him so he could look at her face, his hands resting on her shoulders.

"You should not be here. Things have not gone as well as we had hoped. Only some of the men have agreed to accept our gift and make peace with our kingdom! It looks like the others may attack us!"

"Robert," Lillian said, breathless from the excitement of all that her brother had told her and remembering the information she had to share.

"Look!" She held up the message, "Allia has sent us a word of warning about the Oblager ships. The message must have gotten lost on its way to us, but here it is. They report seven ships making their way to us. How many of the Oblager ships are in port right now?"

Prince Samuel joined them and hugged his sister. "What are you doing here?"

"I brought an important message that you all need to see. It's about the Oblager ships, it says there are *seven* ships, but I only count six out there in the bay!"

Lillian was peering past her brothers through the other side of the tent down to the water to count the ships.

"Right, Malaya already told us about the other ship. But, does the note give any idea as to what they plan to use the ship *for*?"

The princess shook her head.

Prince Robert finished reading the message for the second time before looking up.

"There are six ships at the port but, like Samuel said, we know that they have one ship in reserve."

Lady Susan wasn't as calm as her young royal charges.

"Where are Sir Francis and Sir Edward?" She asked.

Prince Robert pointed to the tent directly behind him. "They are with Lady Dori talking with Silas and a few of his men."

Lady Susan walked with long strides toward the Doyen's tent. After a moment's hesitation Prince Robert and Princess Lillian looked at one another then followed quickly behind their lady.

When they entered the tent the men all bowed to them.

"My lady," they said to acknowledge Lady Susan.

"We were just discussing what we might expect from Erik as we help Silas and his people settle onto the Isle of Drepos," Sir Edward explained to get everyone caught up on the conversation.

"I believe Erik plans to take a ship and leave," Silas offered.

Lady Susan looked briefly at Prince Robert for permission to speak. He gave her a nod, as if he already knew what she intended to say.

Lady Susan approached Silas, taking several steps toward the man and asked, "Where is your seventh ship?"

Silas looked to Prince Robert who inclined his head, inviting the man to answer the question.

Silas turned back to Lady Susan and said, "We had to leave it just north of Allia. It is being repaired."

Lady Susan looked to Prince Robert then at Sir Logan and raised her eyebrows.

"What I am telling you is the truth!"

Silas made a motion toward Prince Robert to plead with him but Sir Logan stepped in between them and took the prince aside to speak with him privately.

When the guard and the prince returned Silas was visibly upset.

"We will take you at your word, Silas," the prince said. "And we ask that you take your men, women and children to the Isle of Drepos. We want to help you settle as efficiently as possible and only ask that you stay there until Erik can be dealt with."

Silas' eyes grew wide and he looked from Prince Robert to Sir Logan and back again. "You won't hurt him, will you? We will not fight against you and we will go to the island as you request. But I ask that you do not hurt Erik or those remaining with him."

Prince Robert waited for Sir Logan to respond to the man.

"We cannot guarantee their safety if they take up arms against us."

Silas again looked as if he would weep. Lady Dori took a step toward him and rested a soft hand on his shoulder.

This was not part of the plan. The gift, why won't the young people accept the gift, she wondered, trying to hold back her own tears of compassion threatening to spill out onto her cheeks.

"That is all, Silas. You had better go and make arrangements so that you will not be sailing in the dark."

He looked up at them, his face sad, eyes shining.

"We are used to sailing in the dark," he said before turning to leave.

CHAPTER NINETEEN

Not long after Silas had returned to the port, four of the Oblager ships began to pull away from the docks, out of the bay and into the open sea toward Drepos. Princess Lillian breathed a sigh of relief and returned to the tent to inform the others. Sir Logan was standing very near to her and she almost ran into him when she turned.

"They are going," he said to her, "but the danger has not yet passed."

She nodded her understanding and allowed him to escort her back to the tent.

"Silas has taken four ships with him," Sir Logan reported to Prince Robert and Prince Samuel who were seated at the table eating lunch with the Ladies Susan and Dori.

"Come eat," Prince Robert instructed, "there is no way of knowing what the day will bring and when we might have our next meal."

Obediently, Princess Lillian sat and began to eat the food put before her. Sir Logan popped part of a biscuit into his mouth and remained standing, nodding to a couple of his men who quickly moved to the entrance of the tent to stand guard.

"As soon as we are done eating, Lillian, you must return to the castle where you will be safe!" Robert instructed his sister, holding one of her hands in both of his. "We have never known a time like this in our lives. We must take every precaution."

Lillian looked into the eyes of her brother staring at her intently. He looked so much older than he had just a few months before, less pained by anxiety yet aged by the weight of his responsibilities.

She nodded in response to his command.

"I will go."

Lady Susan put a protective arm across the princess's shoulders.

"I should never have let you come," the lady said this more to her prince than to the princess herself.

"Lady Susan, I know my sister. I am sure you tried to urge her to stay at the castle, just as I am sure nothing you would or could have said would have kept her there once she had decided she needed to be the one to deliver this message."

Lady Susan smiled, a pink rising up in her cheeks.

"It was important news, wasn't it?" Lillian asked her brother. "I knew it was."

"It was important news, Lillian. But your safety is what is more so. Now it is of utmost importance that you leave this place and remain in the castle with gates firmly closed until you receive word from either Theodore or myself. Samuel will be headed to Allia as soon as you are gone."

"Allia?"

"If the missing ship is to side with Erik we will need all the help we can get. Allia has offered itself to us as an ally. I intend to capitalize on that, but sending a dove will not inspire men to take up arms or sail to our aid. This is a request that must be made in person. I would go myself if the situation here were not so dire."

Prince Robert pulled his sister into a hug as a father might hug his daughter.

"It is time for you to go. Be safe, Lillian."

He kissed her forehead then looked at Lady Susan.

"Lady Susan, if you continue to ride until you are home you will make it just after dark."

Lady Susan nodded.

The three walked over to Temperance and Solicitude, both of whom were ready to ride.

"We will not stop until we are safely within the walls of Castle Grange," Temperance said without Prince Robert having to repeat his directions.

Robert caressed the Cheval's jaw and held there for a moment.

"We need you now like never before," he said and Temperance neighed softly.

Without another word Lady Susan and Princess Lillian mounted their Cheval and galloped toward the road back to Castle Grange.

The rest of the afternoon at the port was a flurry of activity and yet Prince Robert felt like he was standing still or trying to run in water that was waist deep. Everything was moving in slow motion. He was waiting on word from the armory as to whether or not weapons were ready to be distributed. He was waiting for Samuel to prepare for his trip to Allia. He was waiting for a report from Sir Logan. He was waiting to see what Erik was going to do. It seemed like there was much that needed to be done, and yet he found himself *waiting*.

CHAPTER TWENTY

Night fell faster than anticipated and while they had been riding at a steady pace Temperance could sense that her nerves were tense. She did not like being so far from the castle with just Lady Susan, Solicitude and Princess Lillian, no guards, no muscle, no one…

Princess Lillian felt the tension and lowered her body to be closer to the Cheval's.

Lady Susan shouted over the sound of pounding hooves, "It shouldn't be long now before we reach the edge of the woods - the last stretch home!"

Princess Lillian knew her lady was trying to sound strong and confident but could hear the waiver in her voice nonetheless.

"I can't remember a night this dark," Princess Lillian replied, acknowledging her own discomfort without sounding too frightened.

They rode on in silence as they drew closer to the deeper dark of the forest ahead of them.

Almost home, Lillian thought to herself, as if praying it to be so.

She didn't know why she was so frightened. They were far from the port now, far from the Oblager and all of the angry men she had seen at the camp. But still…

Solicitude slowed her gallop to a trot and breathed, "My ladies, we need to slow our pace as we enter into the dark forest. For safety sake we need a moment to adjust to the darkness."

Temperance slowed her pace in time with Solicitude and reassured her girl, almost breathlessly. Lillian acknowledged the encouragement from her horse with a hand on the Cheval's neck.

As they entered the woods the trot of the Cheval was slowed even more. Princess Lillian could feel the cool of the forest lay over her like a damp blanket and she shivered. Her eyes adjusted rather quickly to the deeper darkness of the forest but there was nothing to see other than branches that stuck out over the path.

A squirrel ran in front of them and Temperance jolted to a halt.

Princess Lillian let out an involuntary scream.

"It was a squirrel, my girl. I apologize for startling you!" Temperance said.

The young princess chuckled nervously, "I didn't see it."

Lady Susan and Solicitude moved closer to Temperance and Princess Lillian, close enough for Lady Susan to reach out and touch the princess's arm. She gave it a squeeze before releasing it.

The Cheval moved ahead very slowly. Princess Lillian tried to relax. All of her muscles had tensed in that one moment and now as she began to relax, she felt exhausted all of a sudden. She exhaled and thought she could see a gray cloud of breath leaving her. It was getting very cold. Princess Lillian leaned nearer to Temperance again, this time for warmth. She rested her head on the Cheval's mane and relaxed so that her body moved when the horse did. In a way it was soothing and very soon she found herself fighting to keep her eyes open.

The sounds of the night seemed louder as visibility was so poor in the darkness. The chirp of crickets and frogs rung out into the night, and Princess Lillian was certain she heard the hooting of an owl as well. She listened to the sound of her breathing inside her head, felt it down into her belly and back out again. The sounds, the rhythms were peaceful and she allowed her eyes to close.

Princess Lillian awoke with a jerk. Temperance had stopped so quickly that it jarred her and threw her limp body forward, almost completely over the head of the Cheval. She slid back down the broad neck and sat upright in her saddle trying to look around her and shake off the confusion that lies in between asleep and awake.

"Get back, you!" Lady Susan was shouting.

Who is she talking to? Princess Lillian couldn't see. *Is there an animal in the way again?*

"Get back!"

It was Lady Susan again, shouting.

"Easy now, m'lady," a gruff voice responded, "easy now."

Princess Lillian was wide awake in an instant. She could see, even in the darkness, a man was standing in the way of Solicitude and the Cheval could not move forward. Lady Susan was trying to kick at the man while holding an arm out as if to shield the princess.

Temperance was backing up and closer to Solicitude until the two Cheval were actually touching in the rear. It wasn't until the two Cheval bumped into one another and Lillian tried to lead Temperance aside that she realized someone had ahold of them too.

"No worries now, Princess, we're just going to take you for a little ride," a younger man with a strange accent was speaking to her and grabbing ahold of her arm. Temperance bucked and pulled away, once again butting into Solicitude and causing Lady Susan to screech in anger.

Just as Temperance had bucked again and pushed enough to free them of the young man's grip two more men came up behind them, preventing their escape.

"Your lady can go home, but we need you to come with us," another man said, pulling Princess Lillian with such force she slid right out of her saddle and fell into a heap on the ground.

"Hey!" Lady Susan yelled, running out of words, which under other circumstances would have been remarkable. "That is *our* princess! Leave her alone! If you care about your own safety and that of your people you will put the princess back in her saddle and let us go on our way!"

"Mistress, you know we can't do that," the man who had been holding Solicitude said looking up at Lady Susan. In the next instance he smacked Solicitude on the backside startling her and sending her into a gallop.

Princess Lillian shot up from the ground and ran to Temperance's side. Before she could climb back into the saddle two men had her in their grasp. In the time it took Solicitude and Lady Susan to turn back to try to retrieve the princess the men had loaded her onto the back of one of their horses, a non-verbal quartier, and were breaking into a gallop back toward the port.

Princess Lillian sat astride in the saddle in front of a man who smelled like sweat and salt. It was making her choke and she coughed, trying not to throw up from fear. She was having a hard time breathing. She was too shocked to speak. Tears streamed involuntarily down her cheeks as they rode. She thought, maybe hoped, she had caught a glimpse of Temperance galloping behind them but if it had been her, the Cheval had been swallowed up in darkness and was now nowhere to be seen. Lady Susan's shouts could be heard fading into the distance and when they were finally gone Lillian squeezed her eyes shut.

What was happening? What were these men doing? Princess Lillian couldn't make sense of any of it. And as her breath returned to her she tried to steady herself. If she had been exhausted before she felt powerless now. She allowed her body to go limp. She knew she would need to save her strength. This fight was not over yet.

CHAPTER TWENTY-ONE

Prince Robert felt it had been the longest night he had ever lived. He didn't sleep, couldn't have if he had tried. He had summoned the small fleet of ships at his command and was anticipating the army from the garrison and the weapons from the armory to arrive at the port with the light of day. He was not disappointed. As soon as the first rays of sunlight shone over the Beaumere Sea Prince Theodore arrived at the port with a wagon full of bows, arrows and spears. Several men were with him as well, they had come to help distribute and utilize the weapons as needed.

Robert ran to his brother and drew him into a bear hug as soon as he had stepped off the wagon.

"I missed you too," Theodore laughed as he hugged his brother.

Then in a more serious tone he asked, "How are things here?"

Robert looked at him and shook his head.

"I don't know. I feel like I don't know what I'm doing."

The other men joined the two princes and together they decided to leave the weapons where they were until the guards from the garrison made their way to the port. As the young men talked, formulating their plans and strategies for the day ahead, a drumming sound filled the air. It was the sound of pounding hooves and it could be heard even before the horse could be seen.

Prince Theodore was the first to see Temperance galloping bareback into the camp. He was confused by the sight but only for a moment before he realized what this must mean.

"Temperance!" Prince Robert shouted when he saw her. Immediately, he began running toward the Cheval as fast as he could. He knew if Temperance was alone something must've gone wrong.

"Where is she? Where is Lillian?" Prince Robert urged in between gasps of air as soon as he had reached the Cheval.

Temperance breathed heavily as well and shook off the tension she still felt in her flanks.

"They took her," was all Temperance could say between huffs.

Prince Robert turned and looked out at the ships that were just off the port of Falaise Bay.

"They took her?" he repeated as if he could not believe his ears. "They took her."

Prince Robert stood motionless, staring out at the water. An eternity seemed to pass, at least in Prince Theodore's mind, and he grabbed a hold of his brother by both shoulders and shook him.

"They took her," he repeated. "What are we going to do about it?"

Prince Robert did not speak because he had no answers. His thoughts were racing. Everything seemed to be happening so fast now and again he felt as if he were trying to run in water, against the current.

What could be done? What should he do? Thoughts and ideas floated around in his mind but nothing seemed to make sense. Finally, a voice broke through the confusion, a voice that held the hope of a plan, of action.

"They have taken Princess Lillian, Your Grace?" Sir Logan asked to clarify the situation.

Prince Robert just nodded in response.

"Then we cannot fire on the ships."

Prince Robert nodded again.

"How long ago did they take her?" Sir Logan was speaking with Temperance now, taking charge as he could see his prince needed him to do so.

"I've been riding since the darkest hour of night. Two, three hours, maybe?"

Temperance who was usually calm and quiet seemed to be shaken. She had never been separated from her young girl before, had never been too far from the child she had chosen to protect.

"You could not have done anything differently," Sir Logan reassured the Cheval, as if he *too* could read minds.

Temperance lowered her head in response.

"Have we had any news from Malaya since the last report?" Sir Logan asked.

When there was no answer the Captain of the Guard repeated his question.

"Prince Robert, have we had any new reports from Malaya?"

The young prince's brow was furrowed and he was wringing his hands. He shook his head and his eyes met with Sir Logan's. Prince Robert stopped his fidgeting and stood upright.

"We will get her back?" He asked his captain, or the night sky, or the God above, in and around them. Robert grabbed Theodore, hugged him tightly and breathed, "We *must* get her back."

Prince Samuel ran into the clearing. He stopped abruptly at the sight. He looked from Temperance and her empty saddle, to Robert and Theodore locked in an embrace and finally he looked to Sir Logan.

Sir Logan explained, "*They* have taken Princess Lillian and *we* are going to get her back!"

CHAPTER TWENTY-TWO

Time seemed to jerk into high speed. Everything around the young princes became fast and loud. A group of trained soldiers came into view on the road and entered the camp. One of Sir Logan's men was leading them. The whole area was now alive with activity as Sir Logan took charge of the men and began dispatching them to gather this weapon or that, arming themselves in preparation for battle.

Prince Robert tried to tame the surge of urgency he felt in the pit of his stomach. It would do Lillian no good if he made a hasty decision, a decision based in fear rather than wisdom or tactic.

Sir Logan reported that his men were being armed and readied for battle.

"So, what is our move, Sir Logan? How do we get her back?" Prince Robert asked, unsure of himself and still trying to think straight.

"What about Allia?" Lady Dori asked.

She had been very quiet ever since the younger Oblager's rebellion had become apparent. She had placed so much faith in the fact that the group would accept the gift she had offered, the gift Prince Robert and the Kingdom of Monde offered, for a permanent home and for peace. Her disappointment had knocked the wind out of her sails for a time, but she seemed restored and determined now.

Lady Dori was still fighting against disappointment and frustration but continued, "Allia sent us word that the Oblager were nearing our shores. As you said, Prince Robert, this gesture of friendship should not be taken lightly. We are certainly entering a time when we *need* to call on our friends, to forge and strengthen alliances."

Sir Edward and Sir Francis mumbled their agreement with this statement.

"Lady Dori is right," Sir Francis finally said. "If they reached out a hand to us, we should grasp it. Perhaps they would send ships to our aid if approached in the right way."

"It's time for me to go then," Prince Samuel stepped forward. "Let me go to Allia right now and ask them directly if they will come to our aid."

Prince Robert looked at his brother then to Sir Logan.

Sir Edward stepped forward and said, "It is a sound plan. Prince Samuel and Endurance will be the perfect team to seek out this ally for our cause."

"I'd like to take someone with me," Prince Samuel said. "I'd like to take the boy who has been tending the horses here at camp. I think it will be good for me to have a squire."

"The young brown-haired boy?" Sir Edward asked.

Prince Samuel nodded.

Sir Edward continued, "His father is a soldier. I will tell him that you wish for his son to be your squire. It is a great honor for the young lad."

Prince Robert began ringing his hands again. It's what he did when he didn't know what else he should do with them. He was shaking his head without saying anything and Sir Logan noticed.

"The road to Allia is quite safe," he said, speaking softly to his prince. "Prince Samuel and Endurance should not have any trouble on their way."

Prince Robert breathed deeply and relaxed his hands at his side. He looked at Sir Logan and nodded in appreciation.

"Choose your squire and go, Prince Samuel," Prince Robert said, walking over to his brother and taking him into his arms. "Godspeed, my brother."

Prince Samuel, who was not usually one for long hugs, held tightly to his brother.

"Godspeed."

Prince Samuel hugged Prince Theodore goodbye before turning to the group assembled and bowing slightly to wish them all farewell. He went immediately to the hay bales where he knew his squire would be working to have the horses fed.

"You, boy," he said when he saw the dark brown head from behind a pile of hay.

The boy stood up straight and when he saw who was speaking to him, he bowed low until the prince asked him to stand up.

"What is your name?" Prince Samuel asked with a smile.

"Caleb."

"How old are you, Caleb?"

"Nine."

Though the boy was only a few years younger than Prince Samuel himself, he looked much younger. But Samuel was relieved to hear the boy would be old enough to accompany him on the ride to Allia.

"You are good with horses, Caleb. I have seen how well you care for them."

Caleb bowed low once again.

"What would you say if I told you I needed you for a special mission?"

The boy stood up and looked at his prince, eyes wide.

"What would you say if I told you I needed you to be my squire on a trip to Allia?"

The young boy smiled then paused to look around as if searching for something.

Prince Samuel caught on to what the boy was searching for.

"We have told your father that you will be going with me," the prince said. "Why don't you go and say goodbye while I prepare for our journey."

The young boy nodded and ran away as fast as he could toward the camp.

Prince Samuel went and found Endurance with the other Cheval.

"We will be going to Allia," he told his friend.

"Yes." The Cheval did not need an explanation as the thoughts and emotions of all the men in the camp spoke louder than words.

"I have requested Caleb's presence on the journey."

"He is a fine boy, he will make a good squire. What horse will he be riding? One of the quartier, I presume?"

"Yes. He will be riding Lark."

"A fine steed," Endurance confirmed. "Good choice."

"He went to tell his father farewell and then we will be off. I wanted to pack some food for our ride. I don't remember how long it takes to get to Allia, but the sooner we get there the sooner we get Lillian back."

Prince Samuel plopped down on a stump that was near to where they stood, as if he couldn't manage to carry around the weight of his body any longer. He held his head in his hands, arms propped up on his legs. There was so much to do but he felt like he couldn't move.

"Let us pause for a moment before we set off, my young man. Come here and let us spend some time together."

Samuel slowly rose and walked toward his companion, a strong Cheval with an intense jaw line and muscles that rippled beneath the thin layer of skin and hair on his neck. Samuel was impressed by his strength and beauty as if he were seeing the Cheval for the first time.

He moved closer and put his forehead to Endurance's. Neither of them moved but just allowed their breath to mingle, the air between them to close.

The warmth of their closeness could be felt just on the forehead at first, then neck, shoulders and soon Samuel noticed he felt warm all over. He wasn't cold anymore.

Still they stood quietly. Samuel also noticed his muscles weren't tense anymore and he could focus very easily on the rhythm of their breathing, in and out, in and out, smooth and easy. A quiet peace came over him.

This was prierie; the time of silence. These moments when a Cheval and his companion became one in breath and spirit to communicate at the deepest level. It had been so long since he had taken the time for it. He couldn't understand why he had put it off. He *needed* this.

Slowly, the pair took a deep breath together and Samuel placed his palms on either side of Endurance's head in one final breath of prierie. Then the two separated. Samuel bowed to the Cheval then rose and put a kiss on the top of his nose.

Prince Samuel loaded Lark's pack with food and other provisions for travel then as soon as Caleb returned the prince picked him up and put him in his saddle.

The clouds continued to roll in making the midday seem later than it was and even though he knew the dark of night would arrive sooner than he wanted, nothing would keep them from leaving immediately to seek assistance. Lillian was on his heart and mind and he would not stop until he returned with help, would not stop until Lillian was safely back with them where she belonged.

CHAPTER TWENTY-THREE

"Get her on the ship!"

Lillian could hear the voice but in the darkness she could only see the shadow of figures, no faces. The two men who had snatched her off of Temperance's back were holding her now and lifting her off of the horse she'd been riding. Soon her feet were on steady ground but only for a moment as she was escorted up a gangplank onto, what she recognized as, one of the Oblager ships that she had seen just that morning from high on the cliff above.

"Help!" She screamed up at the hills.

A hand clapped over her mouth and laughter came from in front of her on the ship. She looked up to see the dark, red-haired young man she'd seen in the tent during her first visit. The one who had been so forward and familiar with her.

She looked up at him sharply.

"Oooh, Princess," he continued to laugh, holding a lantern up so she could watch her step up, either that or to show her the sneer on his face. "Princess, no one can hear you from here. But please, do feel free to yell as much as you want. It won't bother us."

Princess Lillian snapped her mouth shut and glared at him.

"Right. Put her in the captain's cabin."

Her eyes grew wide but she didn't want to open her mouth again as he had dared her to.

"Don't worry, Princess," he said, answering her unspoken question, "no one will be sleeping there. The cabin is all yours."

The men did as Erik had commanded and put the young princess in the cabin and untied her. One of the men lit the candles in the room before finally leaving her alone, closing and locking the door behind him.

The princess looked around the room. It was barely as long as the bed that had been built into the side of the ship to her right. At the stern, ahead of her, the night was black fading into gray as the sun made its way toward horizon and could be seen through the windows that composed the far side. To her left was a table with a washbasin, candle, loaf of bread and cup of water. The lantern that hung above her head swayed with the gentle movement of the ship.

Princess Lillian determined she wouldn't touch any of it. But her resolve was short-lived as she felt her legs growing weaker with each passing moment. She had tried so hard to stay strong, to steel herself against her captors. Now that she was alone she wanted to let her guard down. She wanted to sleep.

She looked over at the bed then at the door behind her. There was a large keyhole at the base of the knob and she ran to the door to see what she could see through the keyhole. There was nothing but the same darkness that was outside her windows as the lantern had disappeared with the young man somewhere else on the ship. She could hear the faint sound of voices but couldn't make out what anyone was saying.

Suddenly someone very close to her door cleared their throat. Lillian fell onto the floor, startled by the noise. She realized her door was being guarded. While she had no idea how they thought she would be able to escape *out* of the door, she hoped that having a guard also meant that no one would be allowed *in*.

She stood, brushed herself off and reluctantly walked toward the bed. If she hadn't been so tired, so exhausted, she would have stayed sitting on the floor. She lay down on the bed slowly and at first her eyes wouldn't close.

I need to rest up, renew my strength, she reasoned with herself. She gave herself permission to sleep. Very soon her eyes gently closed and she drifted off into a deep, heavy sleep.

Princess Lillian was awakened by a scuffling sound.

She opened her eyes slowly and took a moment to focus them. When she remembered where she was she shot up straight in the bed she was laying on. She hadn't gotten under the covers, hadn't even taken off her shawl, and she drew it around herself tightly now.

Two men had entered the room. One of the men was carrying a tray of food that he promptly set on the table. The other man was munching on an apple just staring at the princess with a vacant grin.

Once the table had been prepared the man who had brought breakfast elbowed the man with the apple in the gut.

"Oooof!" He said scowling at the first man.

"Get out!" He yelled, pushing the man out the door before he could take another bite of his apple. Then he turned to the princess and said, "There's your breakfast, Princess."

He bowed slightly and seemed to blush a bit, then turned and shut the door once again.

Lillian waited until she heard the key turn in the lock before loosening her grip on her shawl. She unfolded her legs and put her feet on the ground. Slowly, she tested her strength. She had felt so weak the night before. Now, after a few hours of rest and sleep she felt sore and achy. Step by step the princess made her way to the breakfast table. No fresh biscuits and honey like she would have had back at the castle, or maybe even up in the tents with her brothers. Plain porridge filled a bowl. Next to it was an apple and a small glass of milk.

Lillian took a deep breath ignoring the food on the table and walked over to the windows to look out. She was surprised to see the ship was very near the shore. This gave her a little bit of hope that she might be rescued or perhaps that she may have a chance to escape and swim to shore. She wasn't sure how far she would be able to swim but she was willing to try her strength and skill if only to get off of the ship.

"Well," she said to herself aloud, "if I'm going to take a swim I'm going to need some strength."

She walked back over to the table and eyed the contents of the tray. The stuff in the bowl did not look appetizing but she decided she was going to eat it anyway.

Princess Lillian had just finished her breakfast and was hoping to take stock of all that her room held when she heard the sound of the key in her door and she ran to the corner of the room, wrapping her shawl tightly around her for comfort. She wished it was armor, but it was all she had so she planned to use it.

The two men who had brought her breakfast had returned. The man who had been staring at her with dark eyes and a smirk on his face approached her and she shrunk as far back as the corner would allow.

The kinder man with the sun-bleached hair stepped forward too, putting his arm on the other man's shoulder.

"Princess, your presence has been requested on deck," he explained, continuing his attempts to hold the other man back.

He only succeeded in slowing him down a bit but soon the darker man had reached the princess and was tying her hands together in front of her.

"Erik wants to see ya on deck alright," he said roughly as he tightened the knot in the rope and pulled on it, yanking the princess out of her nook.

Princess Lillian straightened her posture and held her head high. Her shawl fell to the floor and she tried not to show emotion though she was sad to see her soft armor lying on the cabin floor. She put on the face of confidence when she felt none of it inside.

"You don't need to pull me, sir," she said, making sure her voice did not waiver. "Show me where to go and I will walk there myself."

The man paused, surprised by her words. He bowed slightly and said, "Follow me, Princess."

Princess Lillian was led out of the room and had to practically run to keep up. The rough man slowed his pace as he led her onto the deck of the ship.

Even though the cabin had big windows that let in plenty of light the full blast of the sun in the mid morning sky was shocking for the princesses eyes and she shielded her face from it. She stumbled along the deck, almost blinded by the sun. She didn't have far to go as the cabin was just below the helm; a few steps up and they were in the open air.

When her eyes had finally adjusted to the brightness she put her hands down and looked around. There was not much activity on deck but when she looked up she saw several men standing near the ship's wheel. Among them was the young man who had been so forward with her when she had brought food to the meeting tent on the hill. She knew now that the man's name was Erik.

Erik was a sturdy young man, not thickly built, but strong. He had a fire in his eyes to match the red in his hair. The scowl on his face and the sharp V sketched into his brow made him look fierce and older than he probably was.

Princess Lillian looked away from him. She didn't want him to notice her but it was too late.

"Ah, Princess Lillian. Welcome aboard The Freedom. So glad you could join us."

His voice sang out over the deck and had a tone of pleasantry that his face did not show. He stood looking sternly down at her from where he stood.

"I hope you don't get sea sick, young one. Once we have taken all that we need from your lands we will have a long journey ahead of us."

She tried not to look surprised by his words, but Princess Lillian had never been one who could hide her emotions well.

He laughed and actually had a smile on his face to show for it.

"You look surprised, Princess. Didn't you realize you would be going with us?" He mocked and without waiting for her response, he continued, "In a couple of years you will be old enough to marry and what better way to form an alliance between my people and yours but to create this union, you and I?"

Princess Lillian was speechless. *Is it possible he truly believes this would be a good way to start an alliance?* She thought to herself. *Could he be that mad?*

"I highly doubt my brothers will simply let you sail away with me," Princess Lillian said, once again trying to sound strong even while her stomach was flipping within her. Perhaps it was the effect of the porridge or simply her nerves. Either way, she tried to project her voice well and told herself she was not allowed to throw up.

Erik laughed out loud once more and said, "I highly doubt they have a choice. The princes have no experience with war. Besides, if they have any hope of keeping you safe they will comply with our demands and once our wishes have been met, we will be on our way. It's all very simple."

Princess Lillian shivered involuntarily. In an instant the sun was hidden behind a large, dark cloud. Lillian felt cold and trembled in its shadow. But again, she couldn't be sure if her body was reacting to her nerves or to the sudden drop in temperature. Tiny drops of rain began to fall onto the ship. The rain was cool and a breeze picked up off the tops of the waves and swept over the deck. Her hands were tied in front of her and her shawl was back in the cabin so Princess Lillian looked around for a place of shelter. The men on deck started moving about and Erik was barking orders, his back to her, as if he didn't even remember she was there.

Princess Lillian ducked off to one side of the deck and pressed her back against the side of the ship. She allowed herself to slide down into a seated position and hugged her knees to her chest, hands clasped, still bound at the wrists. She had wedged herself in between two barrels trying to remain propped upright and yet as much out of view as possible. She was feeling weak. How was she supposed to try to escape with her hands tied together, not only that, but her legs and arms still felt limp from the struggle the night before. There was no way she would have the strength to swim.

"*Hey*," a voice whispered from the other side of the barrel. "*Princess!*"

Lillian looked behind the barrel to see a set of steel gray eyes staring at her. It only took her a moment to recognize those eyes.

"Malaya!" The princess couldn't conceal her relief.

"*Shhhh*! Princess, please stay calm. I just wanted you to know you are not alone. I am working on an escape but I need you to be patient. Can you do that?"

"Yes."

"Good. Don't look for me, I will find you. Just keep your head low, do what they tell you and they won't hurt you."

"How can you be sure?" Princess Lillian didn't feel confident in that suggestion.

"He needs you for leverage. And he *does* intend to marry you. He will not harm you."

Princess Lillian's eyes went wide but she checked herself, took a deep breath and said, "I will do what they say and wait for you to come for me."

"Be brave, Princess," the spy said and then was gone as quickly as she had come.

"Come now, Princess," a voice said from above her. It was the rough man who had brought her onto the deck. "Time to go back inside. Seems a storm's coming. We wouldn't want our princess to melt."

He pulled her up by the rope that kept her wrists bound and hurried her back to the cabin, his long strides causing her some difficulty in keeping up. Even though she stumbled she stayed on her feet.

Once back in the cabin he untied her.

"Lunch," he said plainly, pointing to the table.

The door was locked behind him and Lillian sighed a breath of relief. She ran to the corner of the room and picked up her shawl, threw it over her shoulders and hugged it to her chest. She was relieved to be alone once again, relieved to know she had an ally on the ship. She was not alone after all.

CHAPTER TWENTY-FOUR

Prince Robert stood staring off into the darkness of the night. It was a moonless night and so the darkness seemed even darker than usual. The only light that broke into it came from the campfire that was burning out behind him. Lady Dori came to stand by his side. They stood silently for sometime, as if they were watching something that was holding their attention.

Prince Robert shook his head.

"It wasn't supposed to happen this way," he said.

Lady Dori turned to face him as he continued to stare off into the distance.

"You're right," she said. "We had things planned and knew how *we* wanted this issue to be worked out. But even the best laid plans often go awry."

Prince Robert turned toward her and chuckled.

"Lady Dori, if you're trying to cheer me up, you're going to have to do better than that."

She smiled back at him. "I only mean that we plan things, do our best to carry out that plan but the results may or *may not* be to our liking. But that doesn't mean we lose heart and give ourselves over to hopelessness. It only means we must dig deeper inside to find that perfect peace; a peace and a hope that is not dependent upon outward circumstances."

"Is there such a thing?" Prince Robert asked.

Lady Dori put her hands on either side of the prince's face and looked directly at him, then closed her eyes.

"Close your eyes," she said.

He obeyed.

"Now listen to your breathing. Feel each breath as you breathe in and breathe out. This life-giving breath happens without a second thought. So just allow yourself to breathe slowly, understanding that those things that you are concerned about will be worked out. Continue to breathe and allow yourself to reach for, to grasp, that *perfect peace*."

As Prince Robert began breathing on his own, Lady Dori removed her hands from his face and listened as he took several slow, deep breaths. She opened her eyes to look at him. His face was more at ease than it had been when they had started their conversation.

"Can you feel it?" She asked him.

He nodded.

"It is like prierie," he said.

She smiled and agreed.

Long after the fires had died down and the camp was quiet Prince Robert felt drawn to the area near the small patch of trees where the Cheval were gathered. He quickly but silently went and found Ardor. He was breathing deeply as he had when Lady Dori had spoke with him earlier, but the only thing he wanted now was to be near his companion.

When he found the horse, the prince hurried to him and pressed his forehead against Ardor's. He just stood and breathed. The sound of his breath mingled with the sound of Ardor's and there was something so calming about it, like the rhythmic lap of waves as they wash up onto the shore over and over and over again.

No Oblager. No fear. Just breath. Just peace.

When they separated from one another Ardor said, "Finding the peace within you will lead you to the peace you need around you."

The young prince stood still, breathing and deepening the sense of peace he could feel with each breath.

"If you continue to seek this peace it will allow you to see the choices before you and will give you the presence of mind to make those decisions. Living with peace inside of you is most powerful. It empowers you to approach the situations around you in such a way that allows you to choose how you will be *impacted* by them."

After several moments of silence Ardor asked, "Can you feel it?"

Robert took another calming, deep breath knowing he needed it now more than ever. The young prince nodded into the darkness, "I feel it."

THE END

Thank you for reading The Guardian's Gift.

I hope you enjoyed it!
If you did…

Please help other people find this book
by writing an Amazon review.

Sign up for my new releases email on my website so you
know out about the next book as soon as it's available!

And visit my website: SarahFenlonFalk.com

Now keep reading for a preview of
The Path of Endurance,
the next book in the Sage Cheval Series!

THE PATH OF ENDURANCE

With no moon to illuminate the dark of night, the road ahead of the small group seemed to grow darker and darker with each moment causing them to have to slow their pace.

Endurance was setting the pace for Lark, the quartier, and the horses together slowed their gallop to a trot then eventually a slow walk as they had to feel their way forward.

"My young man, I do believe it is time to stop for the night," Endurance instructed Prince Samuel who was not doing a good job of hiding his frustration with the slowed pace.

"We need to keep going. The sooner we get there, the sooner we get help, the sooner we save Lillian!" He said, almost yelling out his words.

"Patience," Endurance breathed, finally stopping on the road and sensing his way toward a clearing to the left of him. "It will do no good if Lark twists an ankle in the darkness. And for as slow as we would have to travel in the veil of night we can more than make up for in the light of day. Please, let us rest."

Samuel conceded the point without a word. He knew Endurance was right but the urgency he felt within his gut made him feel as though he could not stop moving, continuing on toward his goal, toward help for his sister, toward Allia.

Silently, Prince Samuel and his squire Caleb unpacked their provisions for the night and soon a small fire was built and they were eating what little they had portioned for their evening meal. After they were finished and the fire was dying down Samuel sat watching Caleb sleep.

"You should sleep too," Endurance said.

Samuel did not even look at his companion.

Of course I should sleep, he thought to himself, *but how do you expect me to do that?*

"Worrying away the night will not change what has happened today and will leave you ill-equipped for tomorrow," Endurance said, understanding his young man's thoughts. "It will not save your sister. Please, rest as best you can and we will make it to Allia tomorrow."

Samuel lay down and tried for a moment to close his eyes. That feeling in the pit of his stomach was there again, nagging at him, keeping him from sleep. He realized this would be a long night; it would be a long trip. He was also certain that he could not and would not rest until he knew his sister was safe.

Sarah Fenlon Falk loves sunshine, dark chocolate, playing cards, days at the beach and writing!

Her podcast, Storyteller Station, and online community, Storyteller Nation, exist to encourage people, young and younger, to share their stories and creativity.

Sarah lives in Chicagoland with her husband, four sons and therapy dog named Molly.

All of her books (and more!) can be found at sarahfenlonfalk.com or most anywhere you shop for books!

Made in the USA
Lexington, KY
07 December 2019